THE OLD BOYS

A PSYCHOLOGICAL SUSPENSE THRILLER

MARK GILLESPIE

To Dave, Fiona, Michelle, Steven and all the old faces now gone...
shine on you crazy diamonds X

PART I

THE LADS

1

JAY

The Uber pulled up outside Eternity, a five-star Michelin restaurant off Byres Road in the west end of Glasgow.

Jason Green, better known to friends and family as Jay, opened the car door and stepped outside into a freezing cold November evening. The street was busy, full of cars and people but it wasn't as noisy here as it was in the city centre. That suited Jay just fine. His fiancée, Rachel Harrison, exited the Uber behind him and Jay helped her onto the pavement. It felt like winter had arrived early in Glasgow. Six degrees Celsius, often dropping into minus territory overnight. Jay barely noticed the cold. There was a satisfied grin on his face as he glanced through the window into the warm, soft-lit interior of Eternity.

"Easy," he said, threading his arm around Rachel's bicep as they walked towards the door. "There's black ice everywhere. God knows why they haven't put salt down."

Rachel sighed, but slowed down as requested. "I'm pregnant. I'm not an invalid."

"I know that," Jay said, rubbing her belly softly. "Twelve weeks. What size is he now?"

"*She's* the size of a plum."

Rachel leaned in, her red painted lips touching his ear. "You're going to love our child regardless of gender. Aren't you Jay?"

"Of course," Jay said, reaching for the door handle. Of course, he'd never admit to her that there'd be the tiniest pinch of disappointment if their firstborn child wasn't a boy. Rachel didn't need to know that. Besides, Jay knew she was carrying a son in there. Call it male intuition, and that alone was enough to make him the happiest man in the world.

They walked into Eternity, hand in hand.

Jay and Rachel were there to celebrate his recent promotion with Jay's close family. Jay was all dressed up, wearing a sleek black suit, collar open to reveal a deeply tanned neck that wasn't coloured by the Glasgow sun, but by his favourite tanning salon in the southside. There was a small growth of stubble on his face – a handsome face very much in the classical sense: square jawline, piercing blue eyes and symmetry for miles.

Rachel wore a loose-fitting shirt and jeans combo under her black winter coat. She had her high heels on as she often did, refusing to let her 5'7 frame be dwarfed by her 6'2 fiancée.

"I see them," Jay said, pointing towards a large corner table where his family were waiting. "Looks like we're the last ones to arrive."

His parents, Tom and Beatrice Green, were sitting with their backs to the window. There were two empty seats beside them. Jay's younger brother Bob, along with Bob's wife Celia, and their two children, fourteen-year-old Sean and eleven-year-old Kirsty, were sitting on the other side of the table.

Celia waved when she saw them coming. She said something to the others and all heads turned in Jay and Rachel's direction.

"Look at all those wine bottles," Rachel said, giggling into the back of her hand. "I didn't think we were *that* late."

They walked over to the table, smiling.

There was a pungent scent of exotic spices emanating from the kitchen. Only now, as he inhaled deeply, did Jay realise how hungry he was.

"There he is," Tom said, getting to his feet and approaching his eldest son with an outstretched hand. "My son. The Chief Financial Officer of Global Star Incorporated. And his beautiful wife-to-be of course. The mother of my grandson."

Tom's rough voice, the equivalent of a dog barking into a bucket, was loud enough for everyone in the restaurant to hear.

"Hi Dad," Jay said, an embarrassed smile on his face. His old man was pissed already – that much was clear. Knowing him, he'd probably been drinking before leaving the house.

Tom grabbed Jay's hand, pulled him into a tight bear hug. Jay winced at the dizzying smell of alcohol on his dad's breath. It was on his skin too, as if the old man had been dousing himself with Smirnoff instead of Old Spice. The two men were identical in appearance, only Tom was a little greyer, a little heavier around the middle and due to sharing his son's fondness for lying on sunbeds, he looked about ten years older than his sixty-six years.

"Well done son," Beatrice said, giving Jay a hug that was far less traumatising. His mum was a tiny elfin-like woman with short dyed-blond hair and sharp blue eyes. "All those years of climbing the accounting ladder have paid off, eh?"

"Thanks Mum," Jay said, giving her a peck on the cheek. He tasted her perfume, the same scent she'd been wearing since he was a boy.

More hugs were exchanged around the table. Afterwards, everyone sat down.

"We've been waiting to open the champagne," Beatrice said, pointing to a massive bottle of Bollinger in the middle of the table. There was an oversized ribbon tied around its neck. Propped up against the bottle was an A4-sized white envelope with Jay's name on the front, written in black ink. He recognised his mum's familiar, slanted handwriting.

"Aye," Tom said, his beetroot red face grinning. "Been a tough wait. We've had to drink all this wine just to keep us oiled in the meantime, eh?"

Beatrice silenced her husband with a disapproving look.

"How's the writing going Rachel?" Celia asked from across the table. She was leaning gently against Bob, her fingers toying with the stem of her wine glass. Celia was a native Dubliner who'd moved to Glasgow in her late teens to study nursing. Her Irish accent was still perfectly intact after all her years in Scotland.

"Uhh, it's okay," Rachel said, shifting in her seat to get comfortable. "I'm trying to wrap up as many articles as I can before I get too big and everything starts getting harder."

Celia nodded. "Smart girl."

Tom opened the champagne with as much fuss as he could get away with. Once Jay had a glass in hand, he leaned back, taking a sip of the velvety liquid. He soaked up the exotic scents from the kitchen, tolerating the naff cocktail jazz in the background.

When everyone had a glass of something, Tom proposed a toast.

"To my boy, Jay. Congratulations on your promotion son. Hard work pays off – I've been telling you that since you were a wee boy."

Beatrice glanced at Bob across the table. There was a reassuring smile on her face. "We're proud of you both. Jay with his career, Bob, with your job and beautiful family. We couldn't be happier for both our boys."

Tom's arm was wrapped around Jay's shoulder. With his broad grin, he was the picture of a proud father. Jay could feel himself getting drunk on the toxins seeping out of his old man's pores.

He kept smiling. It was a celebration after all.

"Aye, you've really made something of yourself son," Tom said. "Look at you now, eh? Mind you, it didn't always look so rosy, did it? Let's face it – you almost went off the rails after school when you were involved with that...what was his name again?"

"We don't need to bring that up," Beatrice said. Her tone was firm. "That was a long time ago and Jay was a different person back then."

"That's what I'm saying," Tom said, his bleary eyes glued to his eldest son. "He pulled himself back from the brink of being a good-for-nothing layabout, knuckled down, went to night school and turned his life around. Now look at him. He's got a promotion, a wedding and a baby to look forward to."

Jay's smile was beginning to wear thin. He drank some more champagne and wondered why the waiter was taking so long to come over and take their order. Not that anyone at their table had even looked at the menu yet. And it was a

Friday night – the place was packed solid. The staff were overrun.

"How does it feel son?" Beatrice asked.

"What's that?"

"Getting the job."

"Feels great," Jay said, putting a hand on Rachel's leg and giving it a gentle squeeze. She put her hand on top of his and it was still freezing. "Years of performing general accounting duties for Global have been rewarded at long last. Financial planning, budgeting, preparing financial statements, audits and so on – it's taken up a lot of time but it's finally been recognised."

"What do you think kids?" Bob said, leaning towards his two children. "Are you proud of your Uncle Jay?"

Kirsty blushed as everyone turned their attention towards her. She was the shy sibling – the creative, artsy type who was happiest drawing on her iPad and not talking to anyone. Sean, a little more outgoing than his sister, gave a bored shrug of the shoulders.

"What do you do again Uncle Jay?"

Rachel laughed out loud, almost spilling her champagne over her lap.

"Good question Sean. I don't understand what your uncle does either but I suspect it's something *very* boring."

Jay's hand clamped over his mouth, an expression of exaggerated shock. "How dare you people? I've told you before Rachel, we're a worldwide leader in the secure movement and integration of data…"

Rachel's head flopped forward as she pretended to fall asleep. Sean and Kirsty saw it and both burst out laughing.

"I can hear the baby snoring too!" Tom said, guffawing with laughter and pointing at Rachel's belly. "Keep talking like that son and he'll never come out."

"*She*," Rachel corrected.

"Very funny," Jay said, looking around the table. "Laugh it up. My career might not sound very exciting to the layperson but it's paying for one hell of a honeymoon next year."

Beatrice's eyes lit up. "Oh lovely. Where are you two love-birds thinking of going?"

"We're thinking of touring the States for a couple of weeks," Jay said. He spoke casually as if touring America was something he did every other month. One day, maybe it would be. He'd always harboured dreams of moving to the States someday. "Well, as much as we can squeeze in, you know? Before Rachel gets too big to go anywhere. That's including Hawaii. And I'd like to go to Alaska too."

Rachel shivered in her seat. "The bump says no. Far too cold."

Beatrice was staring wide-eyed at her son, her face glowing with pride. "What a whirlwind it's been for you. Promoted last week. Getting married soon. Honeymoon after that and then it's baby-time. Next year's going to be a good one, hmmm?"

Jay and Rachel exchanged loving glances. Finally, her hand was beginning to warm up in his grip.

"I know," Jay said. "Life's good. It's better than good."

A waitress came over to the table and enquired if they were ready to order. When Rachel explained that they hadn't made up their minds yet, the waitress told them she'd be back in a few minutes.

"Congratulations Jay," Bob said, saluting his brother as if they were old army buddies. "I know how hard you've worked for this."

Jay sat up straight, as if caught out by his younger brother.

"Thanks mate."

"I hear it's the Strathmore Academy reunion tomorrow night," Bob said. "Class of '95. Are you going?"

Rachel put a hand over Jay's mouth before he could answer. "Nope, he's not going. He's too scared."

Bob laughed, but looked puzzled. "Scared?"

Rachel nodded. "Uh-huh. Because he was such an arsehole at school. Because everyone hated him, you know?"

Sean looked at his parents with a startled expression as if he couldn't believe what he'd just heard. He giggled over the rim of his Coke glass. "A what? Did you just say that Uncle Jay was an a...?"

"Sean!" Celia said, whipping out a steely-eyed look that told her son to zip it. "That's enough out of you."

The two kids sniggered into the back of their hands.

"Sorry," Rachel said, lowering her voice. She sat forward in her chair. "What I mean Sean, is that from the little your uncle has told me about his school days, I get the impression he wasn't a very nice person to his classmates."

She put a hand to her mouth, blocking Jay's view of her lips. Then she whispered. "*Bit of a bully.*"

It was the first time that Sean appeared interested in the conversation. "Everyone hated you?"

Jay felt a knot tightening in his gut. He knew his mum had to be squirming in her seat too. "They didn't hate me at school. Actually, I was quite popular."

"Well, you were definitely popular with the headmaster," Tom said, sliding his empty champagne glass over the table. "The amount of letters home we got from the rector, Mr Brown. Remember that, Bea?"

Beatrice said nothing.

Jay hoped that would be the end of it but he could feel his brother warming up in his seat. Good old Bob, never missed an opportunity to drag Jay down a rung or two on the ladder. It was bitterness. It was envy, plain and simple. Bob had once been the golden boy of the Green family. A former athletic standout whose promising career as a distance runner had been wiped out by injury in his late teens. After that, business school and a decent career in marketing but Bob had always harboured a strange resentment towards Jay as his older brother had risen from his problematic teens and gone onto a highly successful career in finance. It was as if Bob, regardless of his wife and children, felt his narrative was on a constant downward trend while Jay's was on the rise.

"Well," Bob said, after a sip of champagne. "You *were* an arsehole back then Jay. I was two years below you at school and even I could see it. It's not that people liked you, more that they were afraid *not* to like you."

Bob nudged his son's elbow. He whispered in Sean's ear, but it was loud enough for everyone to hear over the cocktail jazz.

"Your uncle *was* a bit of a bully. Not the worst there's ever been, but..."

Sean's eyes widened. Jay felt his nephew's stare like he would've felt hot needles jabbing at his skin. "Were you a bully?"

"No," Jay said, shaking his head. "I wasn't a bully."

"C'mon mate," Bob said, an irritating grin on his face. "You and your two mates were notorious rascals back in the day. What was it you called yourselves? The Lads, wasn't it?"

Rachel gasped. "The Lads? Oh, I didn't know your wee gang had a name, Jay. You never told me that. The Lads – wow, how original. Is that because you were a group of...lads?"

She laughed and several others around the table joined in.

"Oh, they were a wee gang alright," Bob said, clearly delighting in this unexpected roast of Jay. "A right wee gang of devils. Eh, bro?"

"Okay," Beatrice said, perhaps noticing Jay's growing discomfort. "That's enough now. Bob, stop it please."

Bob shrugged. "We're just pointing out how far he's come over the years. It's a progress report, ha!"

"I want to hear more about the Lads," Rachel said, winking at Jay. She gave him a soft nudge in the ribs.

Bob nodded. He took another sip of champagne and kept talking.

"The Lads were legendary in Strathmore around that time. We're talking early nineties here. Jay and his mates. What were their names again? Iain – I've forgotten his surname. He was a creepy looking guy, big shoulders, big Igor-type face. And then there was Davie Muir – he was pretty cool, looked a bit like Liam Gallagher, eh?"

Jay scratched at the stubble on his chin.

"Aye."

"*Were* you the school bullies?" Sean asked. He looked back and forth between his dad and uncle. It seemed like he wasn't convinced yet.

"No," Jay said. "And it doesn't matter anymore. It was twenty-five-years ago."

"Jay's right," Beatrice said, glaring at her youngest son across the table. "It was a long time ago. We're here to celebrate Jay's promotion, okay? How on earth did we even get onto this subject anyway?"

"The reunion," Rachel said.

Bob nodded. "Guess he's not going."

"I don't want to go to the reunion," Jay said, finishing the last of his champagne. His dad was quick to top up his glass. "What's the point of these school reunions anyway? It's a parade of nostalgia and a waste of a perfectly good night. I mean, c'mon. Seeing a bunch of people who you didn't even like that much in the first place, pretending you're happy to be there when you'd rather be anywhere else. No thanks. Look forward, not back. That's my motto."

Beatrice was smiling again. "Exactly."

"Did you respond to the invitation?" Rachel asked, a mischievous grin on her face.

"I'm not going," Jay said. "It's not like it's a personal invitation anyway. It's a group invite that's getting passed around on Facebook. I don't need to respond."

He could hear Rachel choking back the laughter.

"I'm not going."

Beatrice stood up, glass in hand. She hit a fork off the side of the glass and it made a pinging noise. "How about another toast?"

"Another one?" Bob said.

Beatrice turned towards Jay and Rachel.

"Thank you for making us so proud," she said, her eyes filling up with tears. "Here's to a wonderful boy – a wonderful man. We're so proud of our beautiful family and all the blessings we've received as parents and grandparents. Bob, Celia and the beautiful children. Jay and our lovely Rachel and the beautiful baby she's carrying inside her."

Rachel mouthed the words to Celia across the table.

Beautiful baby girl.

Celia winked in the affirmative.

"Sometimes nice guys do finish first," Jay said, raising his glass towards his mother and father. "It helps when you've got a start like I had. People who love you and believe in you no matter what. And I know I went off the rails for a while back there in my teens. I know I gave you guys some sleep-less nights. But you never gave up on me, so thank you."

"That's my boy," Tom said, pouring out the Bollinger again. Even Rachel, who'd said she was only having one drink, got an unexpected top up. "A winner. It's all about quality of character son. You've always had that. And I'll tell you something else – that's why you got the promotion and it wasn't that Lenny Sanderson idiot you were telling me about."

Jay felt the mood around the table darken.

"Oh God," Rachel said, creasing her face up. "We'll sour the food if we bring Lenny Sanderson into the conversation."

Bob's ears pricked up. "Who's Lenny Sanderson?"

"An arsehole," Tom said, lowering his voice for what felt like the first time that night. "That guy was bang out of order, doing what he did to my son."

"What's all this about?" Celia asked. Her brows arched in confusion as she glanced at the row of people sitting oppo-site. "Why haven't we heard anything about this before?"

Rachel pointed at Sean and Kirsty.

"It's okay," Bob said. "You can talk in front of the kids."

"Lenny Sanderson is your Uncle Jay's rival at work," Rachel said, addressing the kids directly as if they'd been the ones asking the question. "He wanted the same job that Jay wanted. And to make sure he got it, he started spreading lies about Jay around the office. It was all garbage. A load of nonsense, no one believed it."

"Karma's a mirror," Jay said. "Look where he is now. Unemployed."

"He got caught?" Celia asked.

"Yep. Caught and fired."

"What sort of rumours was he spreading?" Bob asked.

Beatrice groaned. "Do we have to go into details?"

"All sorts of slanderous junk," Rachel said. "He was saying that Jay was into hard drugs. That he's having affairs with pretty much all the married women in the office. Muck-spreading."

"Bloody hell," Celia said. "What an eejit."

Jay nodded.

"That's putting it mildly. Lenny Sanderson – he's not a nice human being, no two ways about it. Plenty of rumours going around the office about *him*. I can sum them up in two words. Armed robbery. Supposedly he was involved in lot of shady stuff about ten years back. God knows how he ended up working in our department. Wouldn't surprise me if that guy had a record as long as Great Western Road. Can't say I'm sorry to see the back of him."

"Let's not talk about him anymore," Beatrice said.

"It's funny though," Jay said, ignoring his mother's request. "I swear that tonight..."

Tom frowned. "What is it son? What happened?"

Jay narrowed his eyes. "I think I saw him. We were in the Uber, coming here and after we turned out of our street and drove onto the main street, there he was...it was Lenny."

Rachel frowned. "What? You saw Lenny Sanderson near our house?"

"I don't know for sure. But whoever it was, they looked just like him. Same shape, same intense stare. He was standing on the pavement, this was a five minute walk from home. Looking right at me through the car window."

The table fell silent.

"It was probably just a lookalike," Celia said, waving it off with a shake of the head. "Not surprising he's in your head though after what he's done. *Jaysus*. Sounds like he got what he deserved."

Jay nodded. He picked up the menu, wishing now that he hadn't said anything about what he'd seen. It had worried Rachel and it made him sound a little crazy.

But still...

"Okay everyone," he said, cutting his brain off in mid-thought. "What do you say we order something to eat?"

———

"Your dad was so pissed tonight!" Rachel said, calling to Jay from the bedroom. They'd arrived home from the restaurant ten minutes ago and now Rachel was sitting fully-dressed on the bed, scrolling through Instagram on her phone while Jay staggered into the ensuite bathroom to wash his face and brush his teeth. "That's the most wrecked I've seen him in a while."

"Aye," Jay called back. "He doesn't know when to stop."

"Not like you."

"Exactly."

"Are you going to be long in there?"

"Eh?"

"Are you going to be long?" Rachel asked, raising her voice so he couldn't miss it. "You're worse than a woman when you get in front of the mirror, you know? With your little man-grooming regime."

"I'll be five minutes."

"I'm counting."

"Good luck with that."

Jay was leaning against the sink, staring at his tired reflection in the bathroom mirror. He hadn't realised how drunk he was, not until he'd almost fell out of the Uber after it had pulled up outside the house. Damn it. There was going to be a headache in the morning and ever since he'd passed the age of forty the hangovers had come easier and stuck around longer. Thank God it was Saturday tomorrow. That meant he could flop out on the couch for most of the day.

He leaned closer to the glass. His breath steamed up the mirror and he wiped it clean with his sleeve.

"You're not your dad," Jay said to the bleary-eyed reflection. But when he was this pissed, he might as well have been. God, he looked and sounded so much like Tom. He felt like he *was* his dad, only dressed in younger clothing. He'd only taken off his suit jacket at the door and apart from that, Jay was still fully dressed. A second button was now open at his shirt collar as he encouraged the fresh air, if there was any, to circulate around his body. It was hot inside the house. Bloody hot. Rachel had turned the heating up to full before they'd gone out, ensuring the house would be a furnace by the time they got back. But she was pregnant. If she wanted the house hotter than the fires of Hell, so be it.

He'd be alright in the morning. As long as he remembered to drink plenty of water before crashing out.

Oh Jay boy, you're getting old. Look at you man, you're falling apart. Crumbling like an old building that someone forgot to tear down.

"I'm going downstairs for some water," Rachel yelled, as if reading his mind. "You want me to bring you up a glass?"

"Aye," he croaked back. "Thanks sweetie."

"You're going to need it."

"I know. Make it a big glass, will you?"

He heard her laughing as she went downstairs. Jay felt something rubbing up against his legs. Something warm and soft and purring. The little ginger cat meowed up at him, looking for attention.

"Thanks Bodhi," Jay said, doubling over to stroke the cat.

When he straightened up again, he felt a rush of blood to the head.

"You should have been there tonight," Jay said, as he continued to engage his reflection in a staring contest. "You played your part in getting me that promotion too, you know? Nothing like a good leg rub to get a man through a hard day at work. Those rubs have sustained me wee man. I want you to know that."

He heard the cat trotting out of the bathroom.

"See ya."

Jay pressed his forehead against the cool glass. He saw everything neat and orderly in front of him – two tooth-brushes in one glass, all of Rachel's beauty products, as well as some of his, the soap, everything was lined up in neat rows that made it look like a photograph of a bathroom from a catalogue. There wasn't a single hair or speck of dirt in the sink.

He pointed at himself in the mirror.

"You're an old man. You're boring now and that's okay. All that other shit back in the day, the drugs and stuff, you were young and stupid."

He ran the tap and threw cold water over his face. As was often the case during these quiet moments to himself, Jay's mind drifted back to a decisive moment in his life. *The* decisive moment. It was 1997 and he was a couple of years out of school, his life drifting aimlessly away from him. He was moving in a direction that was causing his parents all kind of worry and sleepless nights. They knew who he was spending time with, not what he was doing. And despite achieving decent grades in his final year, Jay hadn't applied for college or university and he could barely hold down a part-time job at the local B&Q, stacking shelves and pretending he knew something about DIY to the customers.

His main gig, unbeknown to his parents, was dealing weed for a local junkie, Terry Braithwaite. And it was in Braithwaite's house one afternoon that a junkie who went by the nickname of Beano (God knows why), had OD'd on heroin. Right there on Terry's couch.

Jay stared at his reflection. He'd been a different person back then. He should never have got caught up with those people. With that way of life.

The story was that Braithwaite, upon finding Beano OD'ing on his couch, had grabbed his friend by the legs, dragged him through the front door, took him outside and dumped him on the pavement like he was a bag of rubbish. Terry was strung out on skag at the time too and later on, when he realised what he'd done, it was too much. He slit his wrists in the same house where Beano had OD'd. Left a note with one word on it – 'sorry'.

It was heavy shit.

That's when Jay decided to get out of the drugs business for good. He made a dramatic U-turn, propelled by the fear that if things stayed the same, he might end up like Terry or Beano one day. To think that someone could end up like that – it didn't bear thinking about. But Jay still thought about those guys sometimes. Despite his flaws, Terry had been a straight up bloke and Jay had liked him. Not so much with Beano. He was a space cadet cut out of the same cloth as Syd Barrett and all the other classic drug casualties. He was a weird, skeletal guy who, whilst sitting stoned on the floor with his arms tightly wrapped around his knees, would talk about how he was going to break free of society, create a modern utopia, and rid the world of taxes and greed.

It was all drug-fuelled bullshit, of course.

Not long after Beano's fatal overdose in '97, Jay had cut his hair, cleaned up his act and enrolled in night school.

That was the beginning of Jay Green 2.0. And now here he was, on the brink of the best year of his life. At least it would be, as soon as he got this hangover out of the way.

"You're lucky," he whispered to his reflection. "How did you get so lucky?"

He heard a thump from downstairs. This was followed by what sounded like a muffled scream. Then another thump.

At first, Jay wasn't sure if he imagined it. He was pretty drunk after all.

"Rachel?"

Nothing.

"Rachel? Are you okay?"

Jay stepped out of the bathroom, creeping into the bedroom. He was imagining all the worst-case scenarios at once and picking up speed, walked into the hallway.

"Rachel?"

He ran downstairs, almost falling over twice as the staircase wound its way down to the hall. He stopped next to the front door. Breathing heavy. Staring towards the kitchen door on the other end of the hallway.

The house was dark. And eerily silent. Maybe it was the cat – maybe the cat had knocked something over.

"Rachel? Talk to me. Are you okay?"

No answer.

"What the fuck's going on? Why aren't you answering me?"

Jay walked into the kitchen and turned on the light. He saw the Brita jug sitting on the worktop, two empty glasses sitting beside it.

The back door was ajar. Cold air trickled in from outside.

"Rachel, where are you? Why's the back door open?"

Was she outside looking for Bodhi? Nope, she knew the cat was in the house because they'd met him on the way in and then locked the cat door for the night. So why would she go into the back garden?

"What's going on?"

Jay pulled the door further open. He crept outside, wandering down the path, making his way towards the back wall. The path meandered in between two squares of well-maintained grass and there was a variety of pot plants scattered around the area. There was a steel shed to the left and the garage to the right. Beside the garage, a small wooden gate that separated the back garden from the front driveway.

Jay stared down the garden to the back wall. His eyes were adjusting to the darkness.

He saw a shape on the pathway.

No, on the grass. Someone on their back.

It was Rachel.

"Fucking hell!"

Jay's first thought, which wasn't really a thought but an explosion of noise in his head, was that it had something to do with the baby. It was the champagne. That fucking Bollinger had killed his baby. He knew it – she should never have been drinking in the first place. It was his fault. It was his old man's fault.

He ran over to Rachel, dropped down onto his knees and turned her head so that she was facing him. She was out cold – looked like she was asleep.

"Rachel, can you hear me?"

She didn't stir.

"Rachel. Listen to me sweetheart – you're going to be fine. I'm calling an ambulance, okay? Just hold..."

Jay froze like a rabbit in the headlights.

He heard shoes scraping off the path. The sound came

fast and from behind as if someone had been hiding out in the front garden, waiting for Jay to turn his back on them. The bag was over Jay's head before he could stand up, a shopping bag, trapping him in a plastic bubble while another person grabbed his arms and twisted them behind his back. He cried out. The air inside the bag reeked of rotten fruit. He was pulled to his feet. He tried to fight off his captors with his legs, kicking and lashing out. But he was surrounded and there was no power in his kicks, just flimsy blows swatting air. He felt a barrage of blows to the body, to the head. They didn't hurt but he couldn't stop them.

A name flashed through Jay's head.

Lenny Sanderson.

Jay *had* seen him earlier that night. Sanderson had been stalking the house, waiting for them to come back home.

And now what?

Lenny Sanderson had been to prison, so they said in the office. Knew some bad people. Burglary. Armed robbery. What else had he done? What else was he capable of? Jay had taken the CFO job away from Sanderson, who afterwards had been fired because of the muck-spreading campaign that he'd unleashed in a bid to bring Jay down with him. Sanderson had lost his job, perhaps his only chance of making it straight in the world. Now what? Would he resort to old habits?

"Rachel!" Jay yelled.

The words were muffled, buried inside the bag.

"HELP!"

He felt his legs leaving the ground. Felt like he was trapped in a fireman's lift, riding on a giant's shoulders across the garden. Running at full speed. Now they were back inside the house, judging by the sudden pinch of heat.

Through his plastic cage, Jay saw the pale light on the kitchen ceiling. Then it was gone.

His captors were speeding up.

The rich food he'd consumed earlier was swirling around inside his guts. So was the champagne and beer. He couldn't breathe. Couldn't speak. Couldn't plead with Lenny, tell him that he'd give him whatever he wanted.

Outside again. Jay could feel the cold on his legs and what a contrast to the scalding heat inside the house.

They weren't talking, his kidnappers. Weren't communicating with one another in any way that he was aware of. The only thing Jay could hear was the ongoing sound of their shoes on the pavement. On the road. With any luck, they'd slip on the black ice and knock themselves out. It was a longshot but a man could dream.

Kidnapped. He was being kidnapped.

Or worse.

Jay's breathing was quick and shallow. His consciousness was freefalling into the black but he couldn't go out yet. He wanted to call out to Rachel, wanted to believe that she could still hear him and that she was okay. But she was a million miles away.

Holy shit. He was going to die tonight.

Jay grunted as he was thrown down. He fell hard, like a sack of spuds landing on a bed of steel. He heard a door close behind him. Seconds later, the sudden roaring of an engine.

Movement. Again, he felt like he was about to puke.

He just about managed to pull the bag off his head. It was dark.

A gulp of air. And then, he was fading.

———

Jay opened his eyes. He took a moment to adjust to the motion of the vehicle underneath him. Sounded like he was in an old van that was long overdue a service. The driver wasn't holding back either – he was kicking the guts out of it and the vehicle wasn't so much purring as it was coughing down the road. Was he on a motorway?

"Oh God."

His head was splitting. He lifted it off the floor anyway.

It was dark but Jay could see someone leaning over him. Their features were obscured. It was like staring up at a black silhouette of a demon from a night terror.

"Have some water," a man's voice said. The accent was Scottish but it wasn't Glaswegian. Was that a lilt from the north?

Jay felt a hand on the back of his head, gently guiding him up and into a sitting position. Then the rim of the bottle was at his lips and he drank the freezing cold water.

"Sanderson," Jay groaned, water spilling down his chin. "Lenny Sanderson, are you in here? Rachel – where's Rachel?"

"Rachel's okay," the man said. "We gave her something to help her sleep and then we put her back in the house. Back in a nice, warm bed. Your cat's fine too by the way."

Jay didn't know if he believed the speaker. But what choice did he have?

"Why are you doing this to me?" he asked. "What do you want?"

"You'll find out soon enough. Now we've got a long drive ahead of us, Jay. You need to sleep some more, okay? I'm going to get a blanket for you and I'll make sure you're as comfortable as possible. You'll feel better after a good sleep and then you'll be ready."

"Ready? For what?"

"You'll see."

Jay tried to follow the movement inside the van. He winced at the explosion of sharp pain – how was his skull still intact? "I don't want to sleep. I'm not going anywhere. I want to…"

The shadowy figure came closer. Jay felt a sting in the arm.

"Sleep."

Seconds later, he was out cold.

2

IAIN

Iain Lewis looked at the clock. Felt the usual flutter of butterflies in his stomach.

There was a big crowd standing behind the barrier at the international arrivals area in Glasgow Airport. The people gathered there were waiting for the 3.45 pm arrival from JFK, New York. There were a few Americans waiting (Iain could hear their accents) as well as others from England and a few Eastern Europeans by the sound of it. Of course, there were some Scots there too. It was a good mix of people today and Iain liked the Americans especially because they were, more often than not, a loud and demonstrative breed. They let their emotions out in public, unlike the Brits, a much more reserved nation.

Unlike these people, Iain wasn't waiting for anyone. He worked in the WH Smith newsagent located across from arrivals. Right now, he was on his fifteen-minute break.

Iain just liked to watch. He *loved* to watch.

He glanced up at the big screen with the flight details on

it. According to what was printed up there, the New York plane had arrived twelve minutes ahead of schedule. Twelve minutes. Not bad.

"C'mon," he said, glancing up at the screen. He was tapping his shoe off the floor, getting slightly anxious now. It was only a fifteen-minute break after all and he was already two minutes and counting into that.

Iain looked back towards the WH Smith, his place of employment for the past six years. Six years, God! It was a typical mid-sized newsagent in an airport, offering a wide selection of refreshments, magazines and books. There was a small café located beside it that served pretty good coffee and had some nice cakes. Elsewhere, the arrivals area was mostly made up of seats. Today, a young woman was standing outside the café collecting donations for a children's charity. She was quite pretty, Iain thought.

It was just another day at work.

Iain remained on edge. His boss, Neil (aka Hunchback), would give him a hard time if he saw Iain loitering outside the shop like this. Not that he had any right to give Iain a hard time. This was Iain's break and he could stand wherever he wanted. He wasn't in anyone's way and he wasn't blocking the shop entrance. The shelves were stacked, everything was neat and tidy and Helen McDonald, employee of the month two times in a row, was behind the till working her magic with the customers. Talking to strangers, making small talk like it was the easiest thing in the world.

Did Neil know what Iain was doing? What he was *really* doing? The thought unnerved Iain. Sometimes, he thought he saw pity in Neil's eyes along with the usual blank indifference. The indifference, Iain could take. Not the pity.

Four minutes into his break. Where were the passengers

from this plane for God's sake? How long did it take to pick up their bags and go through all the security checks after landing? Twelve minutes early, damn it.

They should be out by now.

Let the show begin.

He twirled his keyring chain around his fingers. That calmed Iain down. Made him think of happier times, both behind and that still lay ahead if he had the balls to do the things he wanted to do. The keyring was a gift that Iain had acquired only recently and yet he treasured it as if it was a sacred family heirloom that went back centuries. It was made of wood, sculpted into the shape of a closed hand clutching a lit candle between the fingers. It was unusual. It was so cool. And it always reminded him of the best thing in his life right now. Reminded him of his...

"Iain?"

He spun around at the mention of his name. Neil Innes was standing at the shop entrance with a puzzled frown on his face. Innes was a colourless man – his skin was a dull, grey colour. Pale blue eyes, full of suspicion. There was a slight curve in his spine that earned him the nickname 'Hunchback' amongst the more immature of his colleagues. Neil's shirt was always freshly ironed and his WH Smith fleece zipped to the collar as if he was always cold. He'd never missed a day of work in all the years that Iain had worked there.

"What are you doing out here?" Neil asked.

Iain shrugged. "Umm..."

"Aren't you supposed to be on your break?"

"I *am* on my break."

Neil shook his head in a *I-don't-understand* gesture. "Eh? Why are you just standing outside the shop?"

"Dunno. I'm just..."

"C'mon son. Take your break out the back like everyone else or go to the café. Take a walk somewhere. You're clogging up the door."

Had there ever been a more punchable face?

"Or better still," Neil said, "get back to work. Okay son?"

Neil had an excruciating habit of calling Iain 'son' and yet he was fifty-four, only ten years older than Iain.

"I'm finished anyway," Iain said, brushing past Neil and walking back into the shop. He took a final look over his shoulder towards arrivals. They were coming through now, the first passengers spilling past the barriers. Iain paused by the nearest shelf, pretended to face up the glossy women's magazines. He watched the travellers, dragging their suitcases behind them. Saw that look in their eyes. Exhausted but excited. The sparkle of anticipation as they searched for their loved ones in the crowd. And the reaction when they saw them. It was gold. Some of them screamed with joy and broke into a world-record breaking sprint, their arms wide open, faces lit up with elation. Some bounced up and down like they were possessed. Others broke down and wept. Iain saw one middle-aged woman with big heart-shaped sunglasses throw herself into the arms of a young woman with huge blond dreadlocks. They sobbed uncontrollably, spinning each other around like they were trying to make themselves sick. It was a noisy, tear-filled collision.

It was the sort of thing that made Iain's dead heart sing.

As usual, it was over so quickly. Before Iain knew it, the travellers and their people were moving on, wheeling their suitcases behind them and looking for the exit. From there, it was off to the car park or the taxi stand or the bus stop. And Iain would never see them again.

Christ, he thought, turning back to the glossy magazines with their bullshit headlines and sensationalist agenda. No wonder Neil thinks you're a fucking weirdo. You *are* a fucking weirdo. Look at yourself man, you're like a serial killer in the making.

Get a grip for God's sake.

A woman walked past him, eyed the magazines and gave Iain a strange look. Iain tried to smile and then hated himself for it. The woman moved on.

Iain kept his strange habits to himself. No one ever asked specifically why he liked to stand outside the arrivals so much, watching reunions and then like a joy-sucking vampire, feed on the second-hand emotions of other people. He knew what they'd say. Sad bastard. Get a life, sad bastard. Get a girlfriend. Get a straitjacket. How could he make them understand? Watching these people, it filled him up at least for a while. Was that really so bad? Soaking up the joy of loved ones reunited, sharing in that moment from the sidelines?

Leech. You're a fucking leech.

Iain went back to work, patting the keyring in his pocket. It was his symbol of hope and it was always close. The keyring was his reminder that things were about to change in his life. Recently, motivated by self-help books and podcasts, he'd forced himself out of his comfort zone. He'd hired a car and taken a solo road trip up north. Away from the city – from *this* city. Away from the noise. Just driving, no destination in mind. He'd been brave. He couldn't articulate what it was he wanted to find up there, but he knew there was nothing left for him in Glasgow anymore. Just a job he hated. His family were dead to him. He needed something else.

Iain grew to love the road trips and now they'd become a regular thing. Every second weekend, and he'd be counting down the days in between.

"Faster Iain," Neil said, watching him from the staff door. That disapproving look was back on his stupid face. "Start opening up those boxes at your feet son. I need that delivery of magazines out on the shelves pronto. Okay?"

Iain's response was a curt nod of the head. God, having to bow down to this wanker every day. It was humiliating.

He used a Stanley knife to slice open the first box, imagining that it was Neil's face. As he pulled the flaps back, he caught a glossy distortion of his reflection on the cover of *TV Choice*. He was a ghost walking. His dirty blond hair was shapeless and he possessed the sort of unhealthy white skin that made it look like he was missing vital nutrients in his diet. Which he probably was.

Get out of Glasgow, he thought. You'll feel better. You'll look better.

He'd grown to love his road trips. Driving across the beautiful, desolate roads and staying overnight in remote villages where no one knew him. He'd spent most of his time in the Wester Ross area in the northwest Highlands. It was a region with very few people and one that Iain had a personal connection to because his father had taken him and his sister Lynn up there on camping trips when they were kids. They were idyllic memories but faded ones.

On those Friday and Saturday nights up in Wester Ross, he'd even summoned up the courage to visit the local pubs by himself. That was a big deal for someone like Iain, walking into a pub by himself. At first, he thought he'd stay in his room or maybe take an evening walk by the water. That kind of thing. But the sound of live music one Saturday night had reeled him in. Still, he was nervous about venturing into these social settings alone. The pubs around there were the sort of crusty watering holes where, at least in Iain's mind, the music would stop dead every time a stranger walked through the door. Cold, unwelcoming stares would greet him. And then they'd pounce.

But it was fine in the end. He'd walked in, bought a drink, sat down at a corner table and watched the live ceilidh band play a blinder of a set. And then, during the gig, he'd even started talking to a woman. She was the one who'd approached him. She was the one who'd invited Iain to join her at a table with a few of her friends. They'd welcomed him with smiles, bought him a drink and Iain had bought them all one back before the band's set was over. The drinks weren't even that expensive up there. He was doing it. Making friends. Connections. Living life. He even put pictures on Facebook, his first status update in years.

The woman's name was Alison. The chemistry between them was undeniable, and it had been from the start.

Things were definitely looking up.

A girl liked him.

Correction – a woman.

Iain had always been a slightly odd-looking person who'd repelled women for the most part. He was short, extremely stocky with those pale, blond features that made him look part-human, part-phantom. Nature had carved his eye sockets too deep into his skull. His posture was defeated. Someone once told him that he could be an extra on *The Walking Dead* without makeup.

He never forgot comments like those, no matter how much time passed. And the people who said them? He never forgot them either

Iain worked the rest of an uneventful shift.

After work, he drove home in his old banger, a 1990 Fiesta XR2i. He loved his car but it was only good for short journeys like going back and forth between work. Anything more and the car felt like it was on life support. It was a thirteen-minute drive east along the M8 to the southside of the city, to Govanhill where Iain had lived in the same one-bedroom flat for the past five years.

Inside the sparsely decorated flat, he took a ready meal out of the freezer and put it in the microwave. He did the same thing every day, whether he was hungry or not. When he heard the microwave ping, Iain took the meal out, grabbed a can of Coke out of the fridge, then sat down on the couch in the living room and turned on the TV. The woman on the six o'clock news was talking about a bomb going off in some Middle Eastern hellhole. The images were dry and depressing. Looked like the sort of place where it never rained.

Iain stared at the screen, then flicked through the channels, trying to find something else. Something dumb and distracting.

In the end, his attention drifted away from the TV. His dinner was cold and neglected on his lap. Outside on the street, he could hear a man and woman arguing about something or nothing. Iain closed his eyes, longing for Wester Ross and the company of his new friends. For the pub up there. For the music. He imagined his future once he'd left Glasgow. What sort of work would he do when he moved up there? It didn't matter. He'd do anything he could to keep a roof over his head and put a bit of food on the table. Shovel shit. More retail work.

Whatever.

As he grew sleepy, Iain thought of Alison. He was so inexperienced with women that he didn't know what to think. It had been at least ten years since Iain had last dated a girl and that was only one night and she'd been off her face with vodka at the time. The sex was awkward to say the least and as Iain recalled, she couldn't get away fast enough in the morning after she'd sobered up. Since then, he'd sort of given up. Until Alison. Now, Iain was willing to take the risk. It felt natural with Alison. She'd even given him her phone number but he was too scared to text in case he came on too strong. He was afraid of getting to know her or more precisely, of her getting to know *him*. He didn't want her to be disappointed. To discover that Iain was the sort of creep who watched other people's reunions at the airport in order to feel something.

He closed his eyes. Saw her running a hand through her red hair. Alison had a beautiful smile. Perfect white teeth. Crystal blue eyes.

Iain stood up, the erection almost cutting a hole through his trousers. He left the TV on, some shitty soap opera, and went to the bathroom where he masturbated frantically into a tissue. Afterwards, he felt like shit. Like he'd cheapened the relationship with Alison.

"Fucking idiot," he hissed at his reflection in the mirror. Ugly. He was so ugly. What a nerve he had calling Neil a hunchback.

After flushing the soiled paper down the toilet, Iain returned to the couch and started picking at the cold food.

The argument outside raged on into the night

————

The next morning at work, Iain took his break to coincide with the arrival of the Dubai flight. He liked Dubai flights because there were people coming in who'd travelled all the way from the likes of Australia and New Zealand, as well as from parts of Far East Asia. People who'd travelled across the entire world to come to Scotland.

Iain stayed clear of the shop this time. Neil was on the morning shift and he was being a grumpy bastard as usual. His eyes were all over Iain like a hawk on a rabbit running across a field. Was Neil really that suspicious? It was like he was waiting to catch Iain with his hand in the till. Stealing chocolate. Stealing books. Stealing something. That look of distrust and suspicion was always in his eyes and it was exhausting for Iain to put up with on a daily basis. Iain fantasised about punching the bastard in the jaw. Sure, he was a little out of shape but he'd been a good fighter back in the day. Twenty odd years ago. There had to be something of the old Iain still there, inside this shambolic adult version.

Maybe on his last day. Maybe he'd challenge Neil to a fight outside and find out for sure.

Iain watched the Dubai reunion but there wasn't much happening and he was too aware of Neil's presence in the background to relax and enjoy it. Afterwards he went back to work, pissed off, unsatisfied. He could feel the anger coming up.

Back in the shop, Iain was helping Billy, a nineteen-year-old sociology student from Maryhill, to unpack the confectionary delivery.

"You going to that school reunion you were telling me about?" Billy asked, running the edge of his Stanley knife over the box.

Iain frowned. "What?"

"No remember? Your school reunion. It's tomorrow, aye?"

"Is it?"

"That's what you told me anyway."

"Don't remember."

But Iain did remember. The Strathmore Academy

reunion, class of '95, was happening at the school tomorrow night. He'd seen the open invitation touted around various social media outlets for weeks. He hadn't RSVP'd. Hadn't done much besides lurk in the comments and click on the profiles of his old classmates, most of who'd already confirmed that they were attending and along with the help of Caps Lock and a dozen exclamation marks, yelled about how excited they were to see everyone again.

No way, Iain thought. He could just imagine the conversation if he showed up, that's if anyone even bothered to talk to him. Especially after the things he'd done at school.

"So what do you do nowadays, Iain?"

"I watch other people at the airport. It's the only way I feel anything anymore."

"So?" Billy asked.

Iain blinked, as if waking up from a dream. "Eh? So what?"

"You going?"

"No."

Billy giggled as he pulled back the flaps to reveal a neatly stacked container of Cadbury's chocolate bars. "Too many bad memories, eh?"

Iain didn't answer.

After he was done helping Billy with the delivery, Iain started facing up the magazines and plugging up any gaps in stock. A couple of times, he had to stop and go to the bathroom. Locking the cubicle door behind him, Iain hammered his fists off the wall and it felt like the airport was trembling under his feet. But it kept the anger at bay, for a while at least.

He had to get out of here. This place, it was killing him.

Back in the shop, as Iain started filling the shelves, he

glanced outside towards the arrivals area. There was someone looking at him.

It was a woman.

She was sitting on a seat nearby, about ten metres away from the entrance to WH Smith. Iain's eyes were drawn towards her. The woman was blonde with a cute, pixie-style haircut and although the hairstyle made her look young, Iain guessed she was probably in her early thirties. She wore a dark winter coat and, on her feet, a pair of bright, funky green Doc Martens. This wasn't the sort of women who'd usually pay any attention to someone like Iain.

He could smell her perfume. Even from inside the shop, Iain was sure of it. A pleasant cocktail of floral fragrances, intermingled with the scent of coffee from the café next door.

What did she want?

Iain glanced at the screen above the arrival barriers. The one o'clock was due in from Dublin soon, but the woman with the pixie haircut was a little early for that. She didn't seem interested in the arrivals and now she'd turned towards him, sitting with her body facing the shop.

Holy shit.

Iain could feel the electricity surging through his veins. Already, he was putting all the newspapers in the wrong places on the shelves. His legs were rubbery. He felt like a boxer who'd been punched in the chin and was out on his feet.

He tried to go about his job but every little action felt ridiculous and meaningless. She was beautiful and *still* looking at him. A half-smile lingered on her face. Was that an invitation to go out there and talk to her?

"Get a grip," he mumbled to himself.

Was he cheating on Alison by flirting with her like this?

Soon afterwards, the Dublin arrivals spilled through the exit. When that happened, the woman got to her feet and walked towards the barrier, slipping through the small, scattered crowd with effortless elegance.

Iain abandoned all pretence of work at that point. Slowly, he approached the shop entrance, his feet scraping off the floor like he'd forgotten how to walk properly.

The woman leaned over the barrier and Iain's heart sank as it became obvious that she was waiting for someone to come off the flight. Every now and then however, she'd glance over her shoulder at Iain. As if checking to see where he was.

He walked out of WH Smith, pulled by a magnetic force towards a crowded arrivals area. Pulled by that sweet floral scent. He wasn't supposed to be here. He wasn't on his break, but he'd forgotten all about his duties. Forgotten about Neil. None of it mattered anymore.

Finally, he thought. Someone had noticed him.

Remember Alison. Aren't you supposed to be in love with her?

Iain stopped, looked back towards the shop. When he turned around again, the pixie-haired woman was exchanging hugs and kisses with three men and another woman who'd stepped off the Dublin flight. Or had they? They didn't seem to have bags. Had they been there in the airport all along?

What did it matter? She'd just been flirting with Iain, that's all. Passing time.

And yet when Iain snapped out of his trance, he realised he'd walked all the way over to the barrier. Christ, now he was standing only a few metres away.

Go back. Now!

The woman with the pixie haircut noticed him for a second time. Iain stopped dead – a prey animal caught out in the open. It was blatantly obvious that he'd followed her from the shop to the barrier.

His blushing intensified.

But the woman's face broke out into a warm smile. It was as if she knew him from somewhere, another life, another time. Not that Iain had any interest in reincarnation. And then, while his heart thumped relentlessly and he stood there awkward and shy, she walked over to him, passing by the other travellers like they didn't exist. It was noisy inside Glasgow Airport. The smell of coffee and baking lingered in the background.

"Hi," said the pixie-haired woman, her hand outstretched. She spoke with a Scottish accent but it wasn't from Glasgow. She sounded like a *teuchter* – someone from the rural Highlands. "How you doing?"

Iain shook her hand, almost pulling it off.

"Hi."

The woman's friends crowded around them both. They were super nice, good-looking and also wanted to shake Iain's hand. It was like he was famous or something and he couldn't get enough of them. What a buzz. The pixie woman came closer and Iain recognised the perfume on her skin from before. It was sweet and intoxicating, swirling above everything else.

"I was watching you at work," the woman said. Her voice was girlish, much younger than Iain had expected. She pointed over to WH Smith. "Do you like your job? Being so close to the possibilities, but never actually going anywhere?"

"What do you mean?" Iain asked.

"Travel, man."

"Eh?"

She pointed to the large windows on the far side of the

arrivals hall. "All those planes out there. Going places, you know? The Americas. Europe. Africa. Asia – the whole world within touching distance and you, stuck in a dingy old WH Smith stacking shelves. Never getting a piece of the action. Seems like a bum deal."

Iain shrugged.

"You don't seem very happy in your job."

"Would you be happy in there?" Iain asked.

"No," the woman said, shaking her head. "That's why I'm not in there."

"Life's short my friend," one of the men said. He was about the same age as the pixie woman, with a curtain of stringy black hair and a thick Grizzly Adams beard. He spoke in an English accent. Yorkshire, perhaps. "If you're not happy doing what you're doing..."

"You should stop doing it," the pixie woman said.

Iain was more than a little taken aback. Who were these people? These were strangers. He'd never met them before and yet they'd seemingly come out of nowhere to address the shortcomings of his existence, to tap at the doubts running wild in the corners of his mind.

"I'm not happy."

There it was. He'd said it.

"Then stop," the woman said. "Seriously man. Walk away before it kills you. That's not bullshit hippie-dippy advice either – what's more practical than the pursuit of happiness?"

The way she was looking at him. That seductive smile. As if it was really that simple to walk away from everything he knew. Iain could feel the beginnings of an erection in his boxer shorts and he hoped to God it wouldn't go full mast or everyone would see it and laugh. But it was the way the pixie-haired woman was looking at him. The same way that

Alison looked at him up in Wester Ross. Like he was desirable.

"What am I supposed to do?" Iain asked, laughing nervously. "I live a few miles away. I work here. This is my life."

"Come with us," the woman said. She was clearly stone-cold serious. "That's how you stop it. We've just arrived in Scotland and we're going to explore from top to bottom. We've got enough money to last a couple of weeks, after that we'll find some temporary work and then move on."

"Come with us," the bearded man said. "New faces are always welcome."

Iain was stunned. "But I'm at work."

The pixie woman smiled.

"It's odd," she said. "Isn't it? This connection you feel to us. I feel it too and that's why I was looking at you in the newsagent. I know that look on your face pal. Here I am, a complete stranger, daring you to do the most reckless thing you've ever done in your life. I've got a feeling you're a good bet though. We've all done it. We've all left something behind. My name's Lisa by the way. See, now I'm not a stranger anymore. Sammy here was working in a pub down in Carlisle, bored out of his tits, rotting from the inside like you are in that newsagent. We got Sammy out when we passed through a couple of years back. Now he's living a much fuller life with us."

Sammy was the Grizzly Adams lookalike. "Best thing I ever did mate. I was scared too, but I did it."

"I can't just walk away. I've got a flat."

Iain was starting to sound like a broken record. Worse, he was clawing at lame excuses. Searching for a reason to stay put.

The woman's eyes narrowed. "Have you got a wife?"

"No."

"Friends. Family? Pets?"

"Nothing."

"You've got a boss though?" the woman said, pointing over Iain's shoulder. "Looks like he's watching you right now."

Iain turned around and saw Neil standing at the shop entrance. Arms folded, a look of disappointment on his face as if he'd just caught his favourite son drunk and urinating against the garden fence at two in the morning. He didn't summon Iain over to the shop. He just stood there, staring at them with his soulless, lizard expression.

Iain cringed. "Fucking hell."

"He looks like a nice guy," one of the other men said. He was clean-shaven, easily the youngest of the bunch at around nineteen or twenty.

"You know," Lisa said, turning her attention back to Iain, "the easiest thing to do now would be to ignore everything we've just said. Turn around and go back to your boss. Easy, right?"

The thought of doing that made Iain feel sick.

"Well it's up to you," Lisa said, taking a backwards step. "Good luck man, I hope you find what you're looking for. We're parked on Level C if you change your mind over the next five or ten minutes. The offer stands – come with us, travel around and then we'll show you our base – it's a little community we've built up over the years. For people like us who've gone off the grid."

And without saying anything else, the group began to walk away. They didn't look back. Didn't wave. Iain was left standing there, surrounded by strangers reuniting with their friends and families off the Dublin flight. But he wasn't paying attention. Not this time.

He felt drunk on the conversation.

It was easily one of the most bizarre encounters that Iain had ever had in his life. Surely any second now, his alarm clock would go off and he'd be lying in bed at home, having dreamed the whole thing. If not, then the universe had thrown him a lifeline and Iain had just thrown it right back in the universe's face.

"Fuck it."

He followed them. Oh God, he felt sick but he was doing this. Leaving his job, his flat, all of it. Leaving it behind.

A voice from behind. "Iain? What are you doing?"

He glanced over his shoulder and saw his boss closing the gap.

"I'm talking to you Iain. I said, where are you going?"

"I'm done."

Neil ran after him. It was a silly run – the grown-up version of the goofy kid who never got picked in gym class. "Iain!"

"I'm leaving," Iain said. How many times before Neil took the hint? "I resign."

Neil grabbed Iain by the shoulder, yanking him off balance. "Are you insane? You can't just walk off like..."

Iain spun around. His hand was cocked back, ready to strike.

"Fuck off!"

It was loud enough for everyone in arrivals to stop what they were doing and take notice. Mobile phones were out in a flash, pointing at Iain and Neil, the cameras hungry for something potentially viral. Out of the corner of his eye, Iain saw Billy standing at the shop entrance, eyes bulging as he watched Iain and Neil square off at the barrier.

"I'm going," Iain said, getting in Neil's face. He could

smell the man's coffee breath. "You can shove your job up your arse."

Neil's face was the colour of beetroot. "What did you say to me?"

"I said, fuck off."

"You're fired – you hear that Iain? You're fired you ungrateful wee shit. Nobody talks to me like that. Go on, get the hell out of my sight."

But Iain was gone already and Neil's voice trailing off in his ears. Dead words, talking to another man in another life. Now he was running through the busy terminal, reborn but petrified because he'd lost sight of Lisa and her friends.

Level C.

He knew the way to Level C, but would they still be there?

Claustrophobic panic rose up inside Iain. It felt like he was trapped inside the airport, the walls closing in all around him. The building was alive and like Neil, it didn't want him to leave. He could still smell his ex-boss's coffee breath and it was making him feel sick.

He turned the corner beside the chemist and saw them again. They were approaching the lifts. Then they were in a lift. Iain waved, called out to them but the doors slid shut and they were gone.

"Wait!"

He pumped his arms and legs as hard as he could, bumping into the people who were stupid enough to get in his way. Their protests fell on deaf ears. Iain felt sick to his stomach. He felt elated.

All he had to do was make it to Level C.

The lift doors were sliding open and Iain threw himself inside just in time. He saw his wide-eyed reflection in the mirror. Sweat poured down his face. His WH Smith shirt was stained with perspiration.

When he reached the right level, Iain stumbled past the opening doors, almost falling out into the car park. He broke into a sprint. Saw Lisa and the rest of the travellers up ahead, standing at the back of a small transit van parked about fifty metres away. Looked like they were loading something into the back. Bags? But they didn't have any bags.

Iain yelled over to them. "Wait for me. I'm coming with you."

Lisa saw him and grinned. Although she didn't look surprised, more like she'd been expecting him to show up. "Changed your mind?"

Iain wiped his glistening forehead with the back of his hand.

"Aye."

He walked closer. Felt like he was going to pass out after all that running.

Iain saw Sammy lean into Lisa's ear and whisper something. Lisa nodded in response. She wasn't smiling anymore.

"Iain," Lisa said, beckoning him forward. "Come here, will you?"

The alarm bells were ringing in Iain's head, but he ignored them. *Turn back, turn back now.* But this was the new Iain and life was going to be an adventure all the way. Freedom. Walking into the unknown. Like he'd done up in Wester Ross and that had worked out great. He looked back, half-expecting to see an enraged Neil chasing after him Terminator-style. Up ahead, a cream-coloured Volvo was backing into a parking space.

Iain's limbs froze.

It had just hit him. The insanity of what he was doing.

Leaving his job? His flat? What about his car and his dream of Wester Ross and a life with Alison? It was like someone had pulled the sheet from his eyes and he saw the madness. There was an avalanche of doubt and down it came, crashing over Iain's head, burying the enthusiasm of seconds earlier.

The woman's head tilted to the side. "What's the matter?"

Iain shook his head. "I can't do this."

"Of course you can."

He took a backwards step. "No."

"Iain…"

"I need to go back to work."

He backpedalled a few more paces, desperate to get out of the car park. He was a coward and he couldn't do it. Now he was desperate for all the things he'd been running away from moments earlier. The job, the flat, the car. What an idiot. As he continued to back off, Iain bumped into something big and solid. Something that felt like a granite statue. Turning around, Iain saw Sammy standing at his back. Somehow the big bearded traveller had managed to get behind him.

Iain blurted out a clumsy apology. "Sorry."

"Get in the van," Sammy said.

Iain's blood froze in his veins. He tried to run but he didn't get very far before he felt those giant arms wrapped around his chest. Not only was Sammy quicker and bigger and younger, but he was far stronger and in better shape than Iain was. With a hand clamped over Iain's mouth, Sammy bundled him into the back of the van with ease. The others were waiting behind the doors. Urging Sammy to hurry up.

"Quick," Lisa snapped.

Iain fell onto the floor of the van. Before he could sit up, he felt something sharp jabbing his arm. He looked up to see Lisa backing away, the needle in hand. She hopped out onto the car park, slammed the doors shut and Iain found himself trapped in the pitch black. With his heart thumping, he heard the others climb into the front. Heard them talking to one another. Lisa was barking out commands.

A second later, the engine growled as it woke up. They were moving.

Iain felt a sudden stab of terror. He was being kidnapped, quite possibly murdered. How could he have fallen for their bullshit? Freedom. The open road. They were baiting him. They were fucking baiting him and he fell for it because he was such a pathetic loser who believed that a beautiful woman like Lisa had seen something special in him. Fuck! He got up and rammed the back doors with his shoulder. When that didn't work, he frantically felt across the metal panel for a handle. He found one, turned it and it was locked.

He kicked the door. The panic swelled inside him.

"Help! Somebody help me."

Then the drowsiness hit. And Iain fell back, landing in the darkness.

3

DAVIE

The London Euston to Glasgow Central train was making good time.

As he sat in the designated wheelchair space, the tip of Davie Muir's nose pressed against the freezing cold glass. He watched tiny water droplets trickle down the window, but he wasn't paying much attention. Instead, Davie was thinking about the big looming shadow waiting for him at the end of the line.

Glasgow.

Just the thought of it was enough to break Davie out into a cold sweat.

It was scheduled to be a five-hour trip, departing Euston at 14.10 and arriving in Glasgow at 19.16.

Not nearly long enough.

The weird thing was that Davie felt like he was both going home and leaving home at the same time. For the past four years, he'd lived in London, specifically Croydon, working as an IT consultant for a major firm south of the river. His wife and children were in London. That's where his friends were. Didn't that make it home? And yet Glasgow, that big ball-ache in the north, still had an almighty hold over Davie Muir.

The scenery distracted him for a while. As the train wound its way past a gorgeous canvas of rolling, snow-sprinkled hills in the Lake District region of northern England, Davie knew he was getting closer to the border. The snow had only appeared in the last half-hour or so. The proper Christmas card snow, not just the occasional scattering here and there. The cold north, bleak and beautiful was beckoning the train forward. Even now, Davie's heart was racing and his palms were damp with sweat. There was no chance of sleeping through the journey, not on this trip.

How long since he'd been back? Three years? He'd called his mum of course, they spoke every week, and there was a What's App group with the extended family. But as his mum always reminded him, talking online wasn't the same thing as having Davie home in person.

Three years, that was too long.

He had to make more of an effort to get up and see her. His mum was in her late seventies now, in good health, but nonetheless how many more visits did he have left, especially if he kept leaving it so long?

If only she lived somewhere else. Anywhere else.

It was only in the privacy of his own thoughts, sitting on a train surrounded by strangers, that Davie could admit how much the city of his birth terrified him. Too many ghosts. Too many sad stories that he'd left behind. *Tried* to leave behind. There was the accident that had put him in the chair of course, that wasn't a particularly happy memory.

But it wasn't just that.

It was school. It was the old days and the boy he'd been, the boy that still haunted the man.

The Class of '95 reunion, taking place tomorrow night, had triggered him. No doubt about that. It had been on Davie's mind ever since he'd first seen the notification floating around on one of the school's Facebook pages. A Strathmore reunion, oh boy. He had no intention of going and yet here he was, making a rare visit home on the day before the event.

Coincidence?

He could always go, couldn't he? Show up at the last minute and see what happened. It had been over twenty years since the Lads had terrorised their classmates in those soulless, white-walled corridors, in the playground, in the classrooms. That was a long time. How bad could it be?

Davie leaned back in the wheelchair. He took several deep breaths like he'd been taught to do when things started to overwhelm him. As he filled his lungs, he listened to the sound of kids laughing elsewhere in the carriage. He heard the chirp of an electronic game. More laughter. Someone was eating crisps through a microphone by the sound of it.

Could he really go back to that school?

He wanted to see those people in the flesh. His old classmates.

Why?

Davie didn't know exactly but he guessed it had some-thing to do with siphoning a crumb of forgiveness out of them. Or maybe letting them kick the shit out of him – of being punished far too late for the things he'd done back in the day. He hadn't exactly been Mister Nice Guy at school and that was putting it mildly.

The Lads.

Three little bastards who'd revelled in a reign of terror at Strathmore for six years. And Davie had been the worst of them all. Of the others, Jason 'Jay' Green, had been nothing but a poser. A smooth talker, good-looking in the traditional sense but not a guy who liked to get his hands dirty. Not if he could help it. And then there was Iain Lewis – the dead eyed heavy. The scary one. The muscle. Iain didn't say much, but he'd been articulate enough with his fists and quick to use them. There'd always been something a little off about Iain. About the way he looked. About the way he acted. Nonetheless, he was a useful guy to have on your side.

Davie had been the brains of the gang. That wasn't a feeble boast on his part – it was how everyone else had labelled him back in the day. *The smart one.* He didn't think of himself as being clever, not then and certainly not now. But Davie was the Lad who picked the targets and the other two, Jay and Iain, tended to follow his lead. The young Davie liked to pretend that their victims deserved the punishment the Lads doled out. It was bullshit. Trying to paint the Lads as some kind of juvenile justice squad, performing some kind of public service. Laughable, it was laughable. Like that time in second year when Gavin Reid, a little guy with spiky ginger hair, had answered every question right in a verbal chemistry test. The obnoxious wee prick loved showing off. He'd gotten on everyone's nerves that day and to the young Davie, who didn't understand chemistry at all, Reid's cockiness was a threat. It was a threat that merited a visit from the Lads after school. Gavin Reid was off for a week after that visit. And wee Reidsy knew better than to tell anyone the truth about what happened, even though most of the other pupils, and perhaps a few of the teachers too, knew who was behind it.

Smart one. My arse.

That was just one example of the shit the Lads pulled back in the day. There were many, many more and they were all filed at the back of Davie's memory, always threatening to spill forth and keep him awake at night. The verbal abuse the Lads had dished out was worse than the physical beatings. God help anyone who was even a little bit overweight, who suffered with acne, who had a limp or a stutter or any kind of minor imperfection that stood out. The Lads would zone in and pounce on every weakness. There was no filter and they held back for nothing and no one.

The distant snow-capped hills were losing Davie's attention.

He shook his head. Maybe it was all ancient history and as usual, he was overthinking things. After all, he was going back to the city where it all happened. School. The accident. No wonder his mind was working overtime. Maybe no one from the Class of '95 gave the Lads a second thought anymore.

Davie fidgeted with the wedding band on his finger. If only he could believe that.

You want to go, he thought, turning back to the winter scenery outside. It had been snowing substantially around the area for several days according to the online weather news. In the UK, autumn was giving way to a winter that was shooting out of the blocks. And it wasn't even December yet.

How would they react to Davie?

The big man, Davie Muir, rolling up in a wheelchair. What then? Would someone lead the charge by mocking him? Asking him if he wanted to dance? Perhaps some of them, their grievances softened by time, would pity his fate.

Most would be cheering. They'd smile to his face and say how nice it was to see him again. In their minds, they'd be letting off fireworks to celebrate, giving thanks to the gods who'd broken their old nemesis's legs. *Fucking karma mate.* Most of his old schoolmates probably knew nothing of Davie's involvement in the horrific Argyle Street lorry incident back in 2014. Sure, they'd seen it on the news, but most of the media coverage back then had focused on the six people who'd died. The injured were too many to count.

No, he couldn't do it. He couldn't go.

Davie was starting to wonder if it was too late to turn back? Get off at the next stop, board the first train back to London. That was a soothing thought. And a tempting one. He could tell everyone that one of his kids was sick. Tell Elena that he just couldn't face it.

Why couldn't his mum have moved to Edinburgh? Stirling? Fife? Aberdeen?

His younger brother, John, was scheduled to pick Davie up at Glasgow Central. From there, they'd drive the seven miles to their mother's flat in Partick. No, Davie thought. He couldn't let his old mum down. He'd go to Glasgow and he'd stick to the plan. Keep his head down, avoid the reunion like it was a gathering of plague victims. It was just a week's visit. What could go wrong in such a short length of time? He'd stay close to his mum. Maybe they'd eat out a little and hopefully, he wouldn't run into any old faces who were in town for the reunion. The week would fly in, then he'd be out of there. Next time, he'd invite his mum down to stay in London. She could stay as long as she wanted.

"Fuck's sake!"

Davie flinched at the sound of a man's voice. There was a series of short thuds that sounded like angry knocking. He looked up and saw a thirty-something man in a wheelchair, ramming the carriage door open with the sole of his shoe. He lashed out, kicking and pushing, until finally the stubborn door swung open. There was some awkward manoeuvring of the chair into the aisle, then he wheeled into the sparsely populated carriage.

"Fucking door man. What's that all about, eh?"

His eyes roamed the surroundings, looking for a connection. Nobody made eye contact. Nobody answered his question.

The newcomer had a bald head and a pencil thin goatee surrounded by dark stubble. He wore a faded blue denim jacket and to Davie's surprise considering how cold it was outside, a pair of black shorts that exposed two wiry, hairless legs. The Adidas Torino trainers on his feet were scuffed and old.

There was a flicker of disappointment on the man's face as he looked around the carriage. Then suspicion, then anger. His eyes were a fast-moving carousel of emotion. He saw Davie sitting nearby and laughed.

"You beat me to the cripple space, eh?"

Davie's eyebrows formed a stiff arch. "Excuse me?"

The man pointed to the wheelchair space at the top of the carriage, currently occupied by Davie's chair. "You claimed it, eh? Got in there before me. Fair play mate, fair play."

He spoke far louder than was required to be heard. He spoke fast too. Davie figured the guy was steaming although he couldn't smell the alcohol vapour that tended to follow random alkies on public transport. Still, it was the safest bet.

"Aye," Davie said, speaking reluctantly. "My wife booked the train for me. I think you're supposed to get in touch twenty-four hours for long journeys like this one. You know, to make sure there's room for the chair."

The man's face, thin and narrow with a hooked nose was a picture of concentration.

"Shite being a cripple, ain't it mate?"

Davie didn't answer.

"Aye," the man said, wheeling his chair closer. "I only got on at the last stop anyway. Thought I'd just turn up and wing it. Know what I mean?"

Davie nodded. Now he could smell the man, although it wasn't alcohol seeping off his skin. It was stale cigarettes. The guy was an ashtray on wheels. Davie had stopped smoking over ten years ago and ever since the smell of smoke made him queasy. This wasn't good, not good at all. There was still at least an hour or two before the train arrived at Central Station.

"The name's Charlie," the man said. "Bald Charlie, that's what they call me. You?"

"Davie."

"You going home, Davie?"

"Eh?"

"Going home mate?" Charlie asked. "That sounds like a weegie accent to me."

Davie shook his head. "I live in London now."

Charlie looked up and down the aisle, his fingers twitching on the padded arms of his wheelchair. "Christ, I'm dying for a fag. Think I'd get away with smoking in here?"

"I'd wait till the next stop if I were you," Davie said. "It's not that far."

Charlie grinned. "Aye, nae bother." He glanced outside for second, took in the scenery and mumbled his appreciation. Then he turned back to Davie, his fingers still drumming on the side of the chair. "Hey, do you know who you look like?"

Davie stared out the window, hoping that Bald Charlie would take the hint. "What's that?"

"I said, do you know who you look like?"

"No."

Charlie spoke rapid-fire without pausing for breath. "Ian Brown. You know, the singer from The Stone Roses? That's who you look like. You've got that gaunt face and the impressive cheekbones, you know what I mean? You're much better dressed though than Brownie, eh? Nice smart shirt and trousers you've got on there. Visiting a woman up there in Glasgow or something? Eh, mate?"

"Aye. My mum."

Charlie winked. "Nice one. Tell you what mate, I could murder a proper beer. A *proper* beer. Have you tasted the piss they're offering on this service? I saw it on the tray when the women went past with the trolley. Fucking Carlsberg mate – can you believe it? Even the Danes don't drink that piss, eh? Guess that's why they export it to everyone else. Fucking Vikings."

Davie felt dizzy. He watched as Bald Charlie reached a hand into his pocket.

"Nae worries mate – you stick with me and I'll see you're alright. I've got a flask in ma pocket right here. You want a wee nip, eh?"

"Nah," Davie said. "You're alright."

Charlie gave up searching for the flask, took his hand out his pocket and started bobbing back and forth in his chair, dancing to the private rave in his head. Davie figured the guy had to be on speed or something.

"Aye, nae bother. Wanna hop off at the next stop? Get a beer or something?"

Davie's eyebrows stood to attention. "My brother's expecting me in Central Station."

"Me too," said Charlie. "Well, my sister's expecting me but she looks like a man so she might as well be my brother. Ha! Who cares? They'll wait for us if we get a later train, won't they? You and me mate, we need to grab a little fun in this life while we can. Look at us. We're cripples. Life owes us, aye?"

Davie frowned. "You're from Glasgow?"

"Nah." Charlie said, his voice going up and down in volume between sentences. "With this accent? I'm from up there." He pointed to the roof of the train. "I'm a Fort William boy but my close family are based around Glasgow these days, you know? Personally speaking, I can't be arsed going back. Routine visits man, you know? They're only going to drag me about the gaff to see the same old faces and that, aye? Then it's the Gallery of Modern Art and a Celtic home match. The usual sympathy tour for the cripple. *We'll take him out. Taking him out – that'll make him happy.* You probably know exactly what I'm saying here, eh Davie boy? Fuck this, fuck all of it and fuck them. Let's get off the train, hit the pub and get rat-arsed drunk. Find some whores or something while we're at it. Maybe we'll get a cripple discount, aye?"

Davie shook his head. "No offence pal. It's just...I'm not really in the mood to talk right now. I'm tired, it's been a busy week at work."

Bald Charlie flinched. "Eh?"

"I don't want to talk to anyone."

"That's a bit rude mate. Seriously, there's no need for that. You know, that's the problem with people nowadays Davie. All they want to do when they go out is sit and stare at their fucking phones and fuck around on anti-social media. Is that what it is? Am I keeping you off Facebook big man? What's wrong with a good old-fashioned conversation?"

"I'm not in the mood," Davie said. "That's still allowed, isn't it?"

"You're not in the mood?"

"No."

"C'mon man. Live a little. Next stop, we'll get off, find a good pub and then we..."

Davie snapped. The polite indifference in his voice was gone, replaced by a vicious warning bark. "I said no. You understand what no means, don't you? Take a hint mate. Fuck off and leave me..."

Bald Charlie's chair raced forward. He vaulted off the seat, throwing himself at Davie and screaming at the top of his voice.

"CRIPPLE FIGHT!"

Davie didn't have time to prepare or stop the attack. There was a massive banging noise inside the carriage. He felt like he'd been hit by a sledgehammer as his chair was tipped off-balance, his back slamming against the wall of the train. Then he was on the floor, Bald Charlie crawling on top of him with a mad look on his face, screaming and cursing and grabbing Davie by the shirt collar. Bouncing him off the floor like Davie was an egg that he was trying to crack open.

Davie hadn't been in any kind of physical alteration for at least fifteen years. What was the last one? A fight in a pub in Merchant City? Lasted about a minute, tops. And he'd never been in a fight with anybody who was as batshit loopy as Bald Charlie clearly was. What had he done to provoke the guy apart from telling him to fuck off? Never fight a crazy person. That was the golden rule of fighting and one that Davie had adhered to all his life, even back in the day, strutting his stuff around the local streets on a Friday and Saturday night, a teenage heavy with a quarter bottle of vodka and ten Regal King Size in his coat pocket.

Crazies don't feel fear or pain like other people. They fight like they've got nothing to lose. And most of them don't.

The two men struggled on the floor. Charlie, despite his scrawny appearance, had all the weight of a silverback gorilla and Davie couldn't get him off.

"What are you doing?" Davie yelled. No answer. He tried to grab Charlie's head and pull it down in order to contain him. But Charlie's neck was slippery with sweat and it evaded Davie's frantic grip. Davie jerked his hips, trying to shake the man off. He tried again. No luck. Charlie was stuck to him like glue. And so was the excruciating stink of cigarette smoke, ramming its way up Davie's nostrils.

Where was everybody else? Why was no one stopping this?

"Prick!" Charlie hissed. "Too good to drink with the likes of me, eh? Think you're too good London boy, aye?"

Davie wrapped his fingers around the back of Charlie's neck. This time, he managed to secure a reliable grip and using his upper body weight, tried to force Charlie off or at least to create enough space to escape. Charlie was all over it. He adjusted position to retain top control each time Davie tried to get out from underneath. It was chess with bodies. And when Charlie adjusted yet again, Davie saw the man's legs move.

His legs moved.

"What the...?"

"Stop this!'

Thundering footsteps approached the two-man skirmish on the carriage floor. Davie felt someone grab his arms and then he was sliding across the floor like a human mop. Someone else dragged Charlie to the opposite side of the carriage. He was still cursing and screaming, calling Davie a *smug prick* and *London boy*. Davie felt someone let go of his arms. It was incredible how exhausted he was after less than a minute of physical exertion. He parked his back against the wall, heart thumping, lungs gasping for air. Looking up, he saw a heavyset ticket inspector with a Tom Selleck moustache, along with two other people, a man and a woman. Passengers, Davie presumed. They'd positioned themselves in the middle of the carriage, looking back and forth between Davie and Charlie like adults who'd just found the kids fighting again.

"What the fuck?" Davie yelled. He pointed at Charlie. "Your legs moved. This guy...I saw this guy's legs move."

The male passenger who'd broken up the fight, a stocky bouncer-type, was shaking his head. His narrow eyes were expressionless.

"I heard everything," he said in grunt-like voice. Sounded like a Birmingham accent. He pointed a fat, nicotine-stained finger at Davie. "This guy right here, he started the whole thing. He was calling the bald guy names. Taunting him – I heard it, yeah?"

Davie's jaw hit the floor. "What? What the fuck are you...?"

The ticket inspector and the blond woman were helping Bald Charlie back into his chair. Charlie was quiet now, his body trembling like he was going cold turkey over there. At the same time, a lone tear ran down his cheek.

"I'm sorry," he said. "We're both to blame, eh mate? Lost control and that, aye?"

Davie shook his head. "Bullshit. I didn't touch him. This guy jumped me – he jumped *me*."

"If he did, you deserved it," the woman said, scolding Davie with her piercing blue eyes. She sounded like a Londoner, a hint of the east end in there. "You didn't have to say those horrible things to him, did you?"

Davie gasped. "Horrible things? What horrible things? I didn't...am I tripping or something?"

"That would be my guess," the woman said. She backed away from Davie like he was a threat. Stood next to bouncer guy. "You're definitely on something. Pills, is it?"

"This is crazy," Davie said, wondering why no one else in the carriage was coming forward to back up his version of events. "What were you guys watching?"

"Maybe we need to find you another seat pal," the ticket inspector said, finally helping Davie back into his chair. Davie sat up straight, watching the four of them – the ticket inspector, the two lying witnesses and Bald Charlie. They were giving him a look as if to imply that he was the trouble-maker. As if he was due everyone an apology.

"I reserved this spot in advance," he said to the inspector, "and I was sitting here minding my own business when this guy showed up and started blabbering in my ear at a hundred miles per hour. Stinking of smoke. Talking shite. I told him I didn't want to talk and he jumped me. That's it – that's what happened."

"You just said his legs moved," the woman said. There was an annoying frown stapled to her face. "What sort of thing is that to say to someone in a wheelchair? You of all people should know better."

"His legs moved," Davie said, pointing at Charlie. "I saw it."

Bald Charlie was sitting upright. Looking as meek as a scolded schoolboy. "I wish mate. Truly, I wish."

The ticket inspector groaned, then glanced up and down the aisle. Davie turned his head to the right. Gave everyone else in the carriage a hard, *where-the-fuck-were-you* stare. They were mostly sitting alone or in pairs. Some of them had cleared out since the fight, that was obvious by the increased number of empty seats. The kids who'd been playing video games were gone and their parents too. The remainder of passengers ignored the bother up front. They continued to stare at their phones, laptops, books or through the window at the pretty scenery. Anything to avoid getting involved.

All except these two strangers, Davie thought.

Two liars.

"It's fine," Bald Charlie said, hands up as if surrendering to the ticket inspector's authority. "We're both to blame, eh mate? That was silly. Loss of temper on both sides, aye? I've got a bad heart – I shouldn't be fighting."

He was smiling at Davie. Trying to be friends.

"Your legs moved."

"Keep it up guys," the ticket inspector said. "And we'll get the police involved at the next stop. Is that what you want?"

"Nothing's going to happen," the bouncer-like witness said with cold, detached certainty. His eyes were on Davie. "I'll make sure of it."

The inspector didn't look convinced. "Gentlemen, I'd advise different carriages for the rest of the journey. But if you're both intent on staying here, I want a healthy distance kept between you. I'll be back soon to check how we're all getting on, okay?"

"All the best," Bald Charlie said, offering his hand. "Thanks for stepping in."

The ticket inspector shook Charlie's hand. Then he was on his way, stepping through the carriage doors without so much as a glance over his shoulder. Davie half-expected him to start running.

"Well," Bald Charlie said, his mouth curling into a wicked grin. "That was fun."

Davie watched the two false witnesses as they took their seats in the row opposite the designated wheelchair space. They sat side by side, like a couple. Surely he'd have remembered them. The guy at least, whose head alone was the size of a beach ball.

"What was that about?" Davie said, glaring at them both. "Why did you tell the guard I started it? That I called him names?"

Their expressions were blank.

"We're not liars," the woman said.

"Then you're both mental," Davie said, tapping a finger off his forehead. He turned to Bald Charlie across the aisle. "You still want this seat? Well, I tell you what *mate*. Even though your legs work perfectly fine, you're welcome to it. Right now, I'd be happy to go somewhere else. Fucking stinks around here."

Davie turned on the power in his chair. He grabbed the joystick, reversed away from the designated space and then steered forward as if to leave the carriage. That's when Bald Charlie, in an old-fashioned manual chair, gripped the wheels and sprang forward, cutting off Davie's retreat.

"Not so fast."

Davie brought the chair to a halt. He held Charlie's wild-eyed stare, the blood still pumping in his veins after the fight. "What now?"

Charlie grinned. "It's like I said before mate. We're getting off at the next stop."

Davie spoke through clenched teeth. "How many times do I have to tell you that I don't want a drink?"

"This isn't about a drink, Davie boy."

"What?"

"It was never about a drink."

It just dawned on Davie that Charlie's voice was different now. It was quieter, more menacing. *He* was different. The look in his eyes was still and wolf-like. He wasn't fidgeting in his seat like a hyperactive child anymore.

"What's going on?" Davie asked. "Who are you?"

"We're not going to Glasgow Central," Bald Charlie said. "You, me and my two friends over there – we're getting off at the next station."

Davie's mind raced through the options. None of them looked promising.

"We know all about you," Bald Charlie said in a growl-like whisper. "Your name is David Greig Muir and you have a very interesting history."

Davie's growing terror rendered him speechless.

Bald Charlie dug a hand deep into the pocket of his shorts. He pulled out an iPhone with a cracked screen. After navigating through the apps, he offered the phone to Davie.

"Take it."

Davie took the phone. Behind the cracked screen, he was looking at a photo of his semi-detached house in Croydon. The one where he'd left his wife and two children on their own.

A shiver ran down his spine.

"Who are you?"

"That's your house, isn't it?" Bald Charlie said. It wasn't really a question, that much was clear. He glanced down the carriage, making sure that everyone else was still minding their own business. "Next photo, Davie Boy."

Davie's thumb swiped left. He recognised the next building too.

"That's your mum's house in Partick," Charlie said. "Isn't it? Your mother, Audrey Muir, lives alone there, right? You and your brother were brought up in that house and that's where your old man, Tommy Muir, lived until the fatal heart attack in 1989. You were just a young lad at the time, aye? About to start secondary school. Must have been hard. Losing your dad all of a sudden like that."

Davie couldn't look anymore. He gave the phone back to Charlie.

"Just tell me. What's this about?"

Charlie smiled. "Elena's in the London house, right? She's a gorgeous woman by the way, she really is. Thomas, your son. Sarah, your daughter. They're both there too, both gorgeous. Don't insult our intelligence by pretending they're anywhere else but home, okay?"

Davie nodded. "They're home."

"And you don't want anything bad to happen to them. Do you? To your beautiful wife and beautiful children."

"No."

Bald Charlie leaned forward. "Good. Now listen up Davie. We'll pull into the next stop in about five minutes time. There's a van waiting for us in the station car park. I want you to leave this train with us quietly and without making a scene, then get in the van and after that, we'll take you where you need to go."

Davie's eyes narrowed. "And where exactly do I need to go?"

"All in good time Davie Boy."

The two witnesses continued to stare across the aisle at

Davie. It was too much – he was burning up. Freaking out at the thought of these people going near his family on either side of the border. The carriage walls seemed narrower. They were like a set of toothless jaws closing in on either side.

"My family are expecting me in Glasgow," Davie said. "You'll never get away with kidnapping me. There are cameras on this train. You've given yourselves away."

Charlie shrugged. "We know all about the cameras."

Davie reached for the wallet in his pocket. "Money? Is that what this is about? You want money? A credit card?"

"No. We don't want money, Davie. Do you think we'd know so much about you if we were just plain old muggers?"

He had a point.

There was a muffled announcement through the speakers that announced the next stop coming up. Not long afterwards, Davie felt the train slowing down. There was a slight screech outside as the driver gradually applied the brakes.

"This is us," Charlie said. "You coming?"

Davie didn't even know what stop they were at. He'd lost all sense of place over the past fifteen minutes.

"Davie?"

"Aye, I'm coming."

The two witnesses stood up, placing themselves behind Bald Charlie's wheelchair. They looked like carers, ready to wheel Charlie off the train.

Charlie pointed to the empty storage space above Davie's head.

"Where's your bag?"

Davie's mind drew a blank. Where *was* his bag? It took him a minute, but then he pointed towards the luggage rack at the end of the aisle. The staff member who'd assisted him at Euston had left his rucksack on one of the shelves at Davie's request.

"We'll pick that up for you on the way out," Charlie said. "You just keep moving, okay? Go where we tell you. Do what we tell you. If everything runs smoothly, I don't make a call to London or Partick, get it?"

"Aye."

Davie felt the panic clawing at his throat. It was getting harder to breathe and he couldn't remember his exercises. "Why are you doing this?"

"You'll see," Charlie said. "It'll all make sense in the end. For now though, it's time to go. There's a long drive ahead of us."

Everything after that was a blur.

Following Charlie's orders, Davie steered his chair down the aisle with the three strangers at the rear. They went to the door where, along with several other passengers, they waited for the train to pull into the next station. The train rolled to a stop. The doors slid open and someone at the station was called to attach the ramp to the exit for the two wheelchairs alighting. When it was done, Davie was first down the ramp and onto the platform, nodding his thanks to the station assistant. He hoped that somehow, the assistant would see the panic in his eyes and translate that into a cry for help.

"To the left," Charlie said, wheeling hard and catching up with Davie. "Then straight on. Down to the ramp that leads to the car par."

Davie felt the cold night air snapping at his skin. His kidnappers followed close behind, giving out directions.

They spent about two minutes getting to the car park where a silver transit van was waiting. The engine was idling. Lights on. Davie, knowing that this was his last chance to avoid being kidnapped, considered yelling for help. But there was no one else in this section of the car park. Didn't matter. He had to go with them. For his family, if nothing else.

He heard the van doors open and slam shut. Saw three men gathered outside the van. Most of them were heavily bearded and dressed in ragged clothes that looked like they hadn't been washed in years.

"Oh shit," he muttered, watching as one of the men fixed a ramp to the back of the van.

"That's for you," Bald Charlie said, pulling up alongside Davie. "Because as you so astutely pointed out earlier Davie Boy, I don't need it." And with a grin, he stood up out of his chair and pointed to the sky. Then he did a little tap dance around Davie's chair.

"Praise Jesus."

Charlie pointed into the back of the van. It resembled a gaping black mouth, ready to gobble someone up. "Your chariot awaits."

Davie hesitated. But there was nothing he could do. They had his wife, kids and mother within touching distance. If going with them meant sparing his people from any involvement in this, then so be it. He wheeled his chair up the metal ramp and into the dark space. He felt a terrible fear – it was the fear of someone who wasn't sure he was ever going to see sunlight again. Let alone his wife and kids.

From the station, Davie could hear the train departing, continuing its journey north towards Glasgow Central. Up there, his brother would be leaving for the station soon. His mother, she'd been so excited when he'd announced the visit. She probably had something cooking. Had some beers in the fridge for him.

Someone grabbed Davie's arm, rolled up his shirt sleeve. He didn't resist. The needle went in, quick and painless.

"Who are you?" he asked, his eyelids getting heavy. "Who are you?"

Bald Charlie's whisper floated in Davie's ear. The words grew thicker and distorted as Davie felt the drug kicking in. "Sleep big man. Get some sleep – you and your friends have got a big day tomorrow."

PART II

THE CABIN

4

JAY

Jay opened his eyes.

There was, for a second or two, a vast array of bright colours dancing in his line of vision. Red, gold and green. It stayed like that for about ten seconds until he blinked furiously, banishing the colours and seeing instead, the crude outline of a room forming.

"Where am I?" he groaned.

He was on his back, sprawled out over a faded cream-coloured couch that felt like it was trying to swallow him. With its tattered edges and tired appearance, the couch looked like it belonged in a junkyard skip. Jay turned his head to the side. He was surrounded by wood-panelled walls and the ceiling was a mess of broken plaster. A giant cobweb was up there in the corner, but no one was home.

"Oh shit."

He gagged on the dry, musty smell of the couch. Maybe it was the room. Smelled like hay, like he'd woken up inside a barn. The curtains on the window were pulled shut, although a tiny chink of light escaped through a small gap. The room was gloomy, not entirely dark.

"Where am I?" he repeated. "Is anyone there?"

Jay lifted his head off the cushion and although it felt like he had a construction crew drilling holes up there, he persevered until he was sitting up straight. The first thing he noticed was an old analogue clock fixed to the wall. It read 7.17am.

He rubbed his eyes. He still wasn't seeing too good.

"How long have I been out?"

There was music playing in the background. It was quiet, the volume turned almost all the way down.

Jay recognised the song. It was 'The Drugs Don't Work' by The Verve.

He stopped rubbing his eyes. Blinked some more and realised that there were two other people in the room with him. Jay flinched, then zoned in. Two men, about his age. Both of them were out cold. One, a blond-haired man, lay on his back on a matching cream couch squeezed tight against the opposite wall. In between the two couches, a scratched, oval-shaped coffee table stood a little lopsided. At one end of the coffee table, there was a dark-haired man in a motorised wheelchair. His head flopped forwards. Eyes shut. Snoring quietly.

Jay inched forward on the couch. His splitting headache took a backseat to his curiosity.

He put his feet on the wooden floor. He was still wearing the shirt, trousers and smart shoes combo he'd worn to dinner in Byres Road last night. At least, Jay hoped it was last night. Depended on how long he'd been out for. He recalled getting home from Eternity about eleven o'clock, being too drunk to take his clothes off before staggering into the bathroom to brush his teeth. Bodhi had rubbed up against his legs. About the same time, Rachel had gone downstairs for a glass of water.

Jay's body tensed.

He saw his pregnant fiancée out cold in the back garden. Then the terrifying sensation of a plastic bag over his head, the air thinning, all rancid and fruity. Of being carried through the house and dumped in a freezing cold van. A man's voice telling Jay that Rachel was alright – that she was in the house. And then, the sting of an injection. Then sleep.

Jay stared at the two men. His gut feeling about their identity was true. And a second closer look hadn't diluted his certainty, only confirmed it.

Davie Muir and Iain Lewis.

Jay stood up, a little wobbly. He sidestepped past the coffee table.

"Davie?"

He put his hand on Davie's shoulder, gave him a gentle shake. "Davie? Wake up mate. Wake up." It took a while for Davie to stir. Slowly, his eyes flickered as if the internal light switch was turning back on. A soft groan. He coughed.

"Uggh."

"Wake up," Jay said.

Davie's eyes stopped rolling around in the sockets and he focused on Jay, who was leaning over him. His face wrinkled up in confusion.

"Jay? Is that you?"

His voice was at best, a hoarse croak.

"It's me Davie," Jay said, taking a step back from the wheelchair. "It's me. Clear the cobwebs mate, I'll be back in a minute."

Jay went over to the couch. He wrapped his arms around Iain's waist like a wrestler and tried to pull him upright into a sitting position. The man weighed a ton. His body wasn't

cooperative either – his limbs rigid like metal. Once Iain was
upright, he slid sideways down the couch and Jay was forced
to repeat the action of straightening him up. Second time,
he finally manoeuvred Iain into a stable position. Thank
God. No way could he have handled a third attempt, not in
this condition.

"Iain. Wake up."

Iain's eyes were sluggish. His forehead covered in stringy,
sweat-soaked blond hair He stared up at Jay like it was the
devil standing over his bed.

"What...?"

"It's okay," Jay said. "You're alright mate. Something
pretty weird has happened. You're here, I'm here and Davie's
here."

"Eh?"

Jay shrugged. "I don't know man. I don't have any
answers to the questions spinning around your head right
now."

None of them had any significant cuts or bruises. Not
bad, Jay thought, recalling the flash beating he'd taken in
the garden last night. Apart from the headache, he was a
little sore around the ribs. Nothing he wouldn't live through.
The grogginess and the slight ache around his joints would
wear off.

He looked at the two men.

What the hell was going on?

Just seeing Davie and Iain, even in their older incarna-
tions, was enough to bring it all flooding back to Jay. Six
years at Strathmore Academy. He and these two men, boys
back then, had reigned supreme over their classmates. Man,
they'd been trouble. They'd taken it too far but that's what
teenagers had a habit of doing. Plus, it was a lifetime ago.

The three men took a while to get their shit together. To

wake up. To process. Gradually they began to stir like a pack of drunken college mates recovering from the bender of all benders.

"My head," Iain groaned. "I don't suppose there's any Ibuprofen in here?"

Jay shook his head. "Doubt it."

"What's going on?" Davie asked. He cleared his throat before continuing. Sounded like he was hacking up a furball. "Jay? Iain? Am I seeing things?"

"I don't know," Jay said, sitting down on the couch again. He rubbed the sore spot near his temple and it only made the pain worse. "We need to put our heads together, figure out what's going on here. Me – I got jumped last night at my house. They put a bag over my head, bundled me into a van and injected me with something. Then I woke up here. What about you guys? Iain?"

Iain didn't answer. He was perched on the edge of the couch, staring wide-eyed at Davie, gawping at the wheelchair.

"Davie?"

Iain looked at Jay. "Did you know about this?"

Jay lowered his head. "Aye, I knew. Someone mentioned it about three or four months after the...well, after it happened. I think it was Linda Gardiner, remember her? Wee blonde lassie, a couple of years below us. Bumped into her and she told me you'd got badly hurt Davie. I was stunned mate. And so, so sorry. I wanted to reach out to you, but I didn't know how to get a hold of you at the time."

"Don't worry about it," Davie said, stretching his neck from side to side. There was a loud popping noise. "I wasn't exactly looking for sympathy back then. Or now."

Jay nodded. "I get it man."

He *had* tried to find Davie after the lorry incident, but

what he didn't share with his old friend was that Jay had no intention of getting in touch. At least, not in person. It wasn't that he didn't sympathise with Davie's plight, of course he did. Davie had been through hell but the two men hadn't seen each other in almost twenty years by that point. The friendship had long since fizzled out and there was no relationship anymore. Jay figured it was more respectful to keep his distance, to send Davie a card and let him get on with his recovery. In the end, he couldn't find an address for Davie and after that? Life got in the way. He kept putting it off until it removed itself from the to-do list.

"What happened?" Iain asked, shaking his head in disbelief.

Davie sighed. "The Argyle Street lorry incident. Back in 2014, remember?"

Iain's face turned chalk white. "No way. You were there?"

"Aye, unfortunately for me."

"I'm sorry man. I had no idea – I'm so..."

"Never mind about the chair," Davie said, cutting the conversation short. "That's the least of my problems right now. I'd say it's the least of *our* problems. What the hell's going on here? And is that The Verve I hear playing?"

"Can you turn the stereo off Iain?" Jay said. "It's on the mantelpiece beside the couch. Off to your right."

Iain nodded. He laboured to his feet and turned off the small Sony stereo with twin speakers. The music cut out, allowing them to hear the wind outside. Jay could also hear a faint tapping noise on the roof. A bird? Iain flopped back onto the couch, looking dizzy and weak. "Is there any water?"

Jay shrugged. "Don't know mate."

"Where are we?" Davie asked, his face creased in confusion. "Are we in a log cabin or something?"

Jay stood up. "Stay there guys. I'll take a quick look."

He walked towards the door, then stepped outside into a dreary wood-panelled hallway. The hall was short and narrow, and it led to a front door at one end and what appeared to be the entrance to a small kitchen at the other. It was freezing in the little shack. Jay could see his misty breath spraying out in front of him. Every step he took made a cracking noise in the floor, in the walls, so loud that it sounded like the building was about to collapse on his head. That earthy hay-like scent was following him too.

He walked around, calling back to the others. "Aye, it's a cabin. Pretty small by the look of it. Hallway leads to the front door. Kitchen to the back. Christ, it stinks out here."

Jay studied a trio of closed doors that lined the hallway. Cupboards? Bedrooms?

"Is there an upstairs?" Davie called from the living room.

"Nope. One-storey."

Jay opened the three doors. "Toilet. Storage cupboard in there too. Here we go – two bedrooms. Oh God, what a mess. Dusty carpets, king sized beds, just the frames and no mattresses. One of the rooms has floor to ceiling windows, curtains closed. The lights seem to work so we're good for electricity. Hang on. What's this? There's a tiny en-suite bathroom in one of the bedrooms and inside...let's see...a shower unit that hasn't been cleaned in years. Jesus, we're drowning in dust."

Satisfied that he hadn't missed any secret rooms, Jay returned to the living room. "They've spared no expense on our accommodation, that's for sure. This place is old and disused."

Davie nodded. "And yet the lights work."

"Who's *they*?" Iain asked. "Who did this to us? Does anybody actually know what's going on here?"

No one had an answer.

"What about those curtains over there?" Davie asked. "Has anyone opened them yet?"

Jay stared at the dusty black curtains. They were as worn down as the couch, hanging off the track like bulky vampire cloaks waiting for a Halloween party. Despite wanting to understand more about their predicament, something was holding Jay back from pulling them open and taking a look outside. It was the obvious thing to do and yet...

"Is the door locked?" Davie asked, jerking a thumb towards the hallway. "Did you try the front door?"

Jay shook his head. "Not yet. Tell you the truth mate, I'm worried what we'll find out there."

He glanced at the other two.

"I don't understand any of this boys. The three of us, kidnapped in separate locations, drugged and dumped in a cabin. Unless that is..."

"What?" Iain asked.

"There's a name in my head," Jay said. "Last night when they jumped me in the garden, there was a name in my head. Lenny Sanderson."

Davie frowned. "Who?"

"He's a guy I pissed off at work," Jay said, sitting on the arm of the couch. As he spoke, he picked at the torn upholstery. "I beat him out of a major promotion last week at Global. A CFO gig. Long story short, he got the axe and he blames me for it. And this isn't a nice guy I'm talking about – there are stories going around work that he's got a criminal background."

"Even so," Davie said. "You think this guy's capable of doing something like this? *This*? Kidnapping you at your house?"

"They bundled me into a van at the airport," Iain said.

"Airport?" Jay asked, getting back to his feet and stretching his limbs. "Were you going somewhere?"

"I work there."

"At the airport? Doing what?"

"I work in the WH Smith."

"The newsagent?"

"Aye."

Jay nodded, tried to look at least slightly interested. "Cool. Well, we'd better start putting our heads together guys. Figure out for sure what this is."

"We're putting our heads together Jay," Davie said. His tone was cutting. "Or hadn't you noticed?"

That stopped Jay in his tracks. Already, he thought, it was starting to feel like the old days. He sensed the old dynamics, slowly reforming. Jay and Davie jousting for control while Iain watched in silence.

"They got me at home," Jay said. "Iain at work. What about you Davie? Where did they grab you?"

"On the train. I was on my way to Central Station when some headcase started a fight with me in the carriage. The guy had a quiet word in my ear. Told me I was getting off the train with him and his buddies at the next stop. They showed me pictures of my mum's house. Of *my* house in London. They knew my wife's name and my children's names for God's sake. Told me what would happen if I didn't cooperate."

Jay shook his head. "Jesus."

"At least it's warm in here," Iain said, pointing at two portable panel heaters sitting on the floor on opposite ends of the room. "They don't want us to freeze to death."

"Uh-huh," Jay said, glancing at the electric heaters. "So, what *do* they want?"

Davie pointed to the window. "We'd better open the curtains."

Jay nodded in agreement. Maybe Davie could take his chair over and do it, seeing as how he was the one barking out the orders. But when no one else moved, Jay groaned and marched over to the window. After a moment's hesitation, he pulled back the thick curtains. Bright light seeped into the living room, far from overwhelming. It was a dull, late autumnal morning out there.

"Can't see much," Jay said, pressing his face against the glass. The glass was a block of solid ice. "We're out in the sticks though, there's no doubt about that. I can't see any other houses or cabins or any buildings. No lights. No roads, can't hear any traffic. I see hills over there in the distance. It's snowing too. Starting to lie on the ground."

"They brought us here overnight," Davie said. "To the middle of nowhere. Why? What are we supposed to do now?"

Iain stood up. "I need water. My head's splitting."

Jay stepped back from the window, pulling the curtains closed again. He felt more secure when they were closed. "Me too. You want a drink Davie?"

"Aye," Davie said. "If there's any water I'll have some."

"Back in a tick mate."

Jay and Iain walked in single file towards the kitchen. At the kitchen doorway, Iain hit the light switch and a pale, unshielded bulb made a scratching noise as it flickered overhead. It was a tired old kitchen. There was an arched fireplace on the far side of the room, a wooden table with benches on the other. A few cooking utensils hung from hooks nailed into a stone wall and nearby, a collage of rusty pots was scattered around the sink. There was no fridge, but several two-litre bottles of water had been left on the table along with a bag of red Royal Gala apples, six bananas, a loaf of bread, a jar of peanut butter and a bottle of Johnnie Walker whisky.

There was also a note on the table.

"Davie!" Jay yelled. "You'd better get your arse in here. Quick as you can, eh? We've found something."

Jay stared at the note, listening to Davie's chair as it raced down the hallway like an F1 car towards the finish line. Davie hurried through the open doorway, pulling up beside the kitchen table. His eyes widened in anticipation.

"What is it?"

"There's a note," Jay said, picking up the slip of paper. His hand was surprisingly steady.

"Oh shit," Davie said, staring at the note. "Here we go then."

Jay scratched at the darkening shadow of stubble on his chin. Felt like there was a day's growth on his face already. He studied the note. "It starts with a list of our names. Then..."

"Read it for fuck's sake," Davie snapped. "Will you just fucking read it from start to finish without the commentary?"

Jay glanced at Davie. "Fine."

He took a deep breath.

"*Jason Green*
Iain Lewis
David Muir
The Lads.
Pay close attention.

Jay hesitated. He glanced at the others, his heart beating like a drum.

'*One of you is a killer. Let me repeat, there's a killer amongst you. Here's what we ask of you – the killer must confess. Confess before sunset and you will all be released, blindfolded and taken back to your lives in the big cities. This is about accountability. You cannot escape from the cabin without a confession. If there is no confession...'*

Jay swallowed.

'...you will all die tonight.'

5

IAIN

Iain's headache was getting worse.

He tried to concentrate as Jay read the note for a second time. Or was this the third time already? Didn't matter – the words hadn't changed and neither had the meaning. And yet when each reading was over, Jay would launch into the next one, the panic in his voice getting more obvious every time. Iain didn't understand what Jay was doing. It was as if the poor bastard was convinced there was a punchline that he kept missing.

Eventually, Jay put the note down on the table. Iain watched him and it was like looking at a man who'd just been informed that his entire family had died in a plane crash. He looked older than Iain had ever imagined seeing Jay. The man was stunned into silence. They all were. Nobody spoke for at least a minute or two after the note had been read out at least six times. The three men just stayed put, eyeing one another warily across the kitchen table.

Cold air seeped into the house. Iain felt it running down the back of his neck, causing him to flinch.

Now it was Davie's turn to pick up the note. His eyes ran up and down the black, slanted ink. "That looks like a woman's handwriting."

"How can you tell?" Iain asked.

"I mean, it's not bulletproof logic or anything. But women's handwriting is usually more curved, the letters bowed out like they are here. See?"

"Confess?" Jay said, staring at the piece of paper in Davie's hand. "They're asking for a confession. According to them, one of us is a..."

He threw a suspicious glance at the other two men.

"Well, it says it right there on the page."

"I didn't do anything," Iain said, blurting it out too fast. He didn't like the way that Jay and Davie's eyes kept coming back to him. They weren't looking at each other, not in the same way they were staring at him. No surprise, of course. They'd already pegged him as guilty.

Jay scratched his chin. The grating sound of the man's fingernails raking up and down the stubble was excruciating.

"There must be a mistake," Jay said, his eyes scanning the corners of the walls and ceiling. Iain guessed that Jay was searching for some kind of hidden surveillance. "Now, straight off the bat, let's just lay it out there. Killer? I haven't killed anyone. Davie? Have you killed anyone recently?"

Davie shook his head. "Not that I know of."

Jay nodded. "Okay. Iain?"

Iain's fingers curled into the palms of his hands. He felt the nails slice into his flesh and he pushed them in deeper. "I just told you. It wasn't me."

That fucking smug look on Jay's face. It hadn't changed much in twenty-five years, except there were a few more wrinkles around the eyes. And that tan – who the hell did he think he was? Don Johnson in *Miami Vice*?

"No offence mate," Jay said, pointing at the note that Davie had put back on the table. "Listen, I'm not saying you're a killer. Hell, I'm not saying anyone here's a killer – it's a ludicrous idea. But look at that. There's a note on the table with our names on it. We've been kidnapped for God's sake. People don't go to these lengths for nothing."

"Unless it's a mistake," Davie said. "I don't know. Mistaken identity or something like that?"

"All three of us?" Jay asked.

"Aye, maybe not."

Jay grabbed the note. He read it quietly to himself this time and then slammed it back down on the table. "No, whatever this is – it's not a mistake. This was organised. This was methodical and it's pretty clear from the way they grabbed us that they've been watching us. Probably for some time."

Jay glanced at Iain again. Iain looked away. It felt to Iain like Jay was a cop sitting across from a suspect in the interrogation room, turning up the heat, waiting for the inevitable confession regardless of the suspect's guilt or innocence.

"Fuck off Jay," Iain growled. "I see you looking at me."

Jay held up his hands. Looked at Davie, then back at Iain. "What's the matter with you for God's sake?"

"Stop looking at me like that," Iain said. "I know you think it's me."

"Enough for Christ's sake."

Davie drove his chair into the centre of the kitchen and with a sweeping hand gesture, signalled for calm. "Enough.

Take it easy. This is a lot to swallow but we can't lose our nerve."

"Tell him to stop looking at me like I'm a murderer," Iain said. "You don't think I see it, Jay?"

"What am I?" Davie said, turning to Iain. "Your mum?"

Jay made a loud tut-tutting noise. He shook his head with an exaggerated look of disappointment. "Same old Iain. Still blaming everyone else for your..."

Davie thumped a fist off the arm of his chair.

"Shut the fuck up you two, will you? We don't have time to fight amongst ourselves." His eyes scanned the room, looking for clues, hints, arrows to the truth – anything that would start making sense of the situation. "Before we do anything else let's just cut to the chase. This is official, on the record. No bullshit, okay?"

Jay and Iain both nodded.

"Deep breaths," Davie said, taking his own advice. "Take a deep breath first and think about your answer to the question."

Iain took a deep breath as instructed. Not because Davie told him to, but because he had to keep it together. Had to keep his emotions in check, no matter how rough it got. He knew that Jay and Davie were waiting for him to crack. Waiting for him confess to something that he hadn't done. History showed that these two didn't give a flying fuck about Iain and would happily throw him to the dogs.

But these weren't the little gods he'd gone to school with. Not anymore.

He couldn't stop looking at Davie in the wheelchair. The great Davie Muir was no more – he'd shrunk into an older, frailer version of himself. Davie had been the coolest kid in their year by far. He'd had everything going for him, except his dad dying when he was twelve. Davie was just as tall as

Jay, well when he was standing up he was. Not as conventionally handsome, but not ugly like Iain. This older version of Davie was different – he was pale and prematurely wrinkled, especially under the eyes where dark shadows lingered. His hair was greying at the sides. His posture, broken and tired.

"Okay," Davie said, glancing around the room. "Here goes. Has anyone here ever killed anyone?"

Jay pulled a chair at the table and sat down. He propped his elbows up on the surface, looked the other two straight in the eyes. "That's a hard no from me."

Iain answered in a gruff voice. "No."

"I'm no murderer either," Davie said, his lips barely moving as he stared at the note. "I've done some shitty things in my life but…"

"The note says killer," Jay said, stabbing the paper with his index finger. "Killer. Not murderer. They're not necessarily one and the same thing."

"Let's just assume the most obvious interpretation," Davie said. "Shall we? I don't think we're here because someone accidentally stepped on an ant. The way I see it, there's two possibilities here. Whoever set this up is playing mind games or…"

"Or what?" Jay asked.

"Or one of us is a liar."

Iain studied both their faces, but he couldn't read them like he could back in the day. He stared longingly at the whisky, a one litre bottle of Johnnie Walker Black Label. It was cold – there were no portable heaters in the kitchen. The whisky was the next best thing they had when it came to keeping warm.

Jay whacked his fist off the table. All of a sudden, he jumped back to his feet and started laughing. It wasn't ordinary laughter – it was the mad-eyed laughter of a man who'd just been taken off death row.

"What the hell's wrong with you?" Davie asked.

"Isn't it obvious? This is a joke, isn't it? It's a wind up."

"Jay," Davie said. "Calm down, will you? It's not a wind-up. Think about it – you got jumped last night. They knocked your wife out…"

"She's not my wife yet," Jay said, grinning. "And if I find out she's involved in this gag, she might never be…"

Davie screwed his face up. "Jay! You got hit over the head, didn't you? You got thrown into the back of a van where you were drugged. They grabbed Iain at the airport. I was on the train – I wasn't even in Scotland yet for God's sake. You really think it's a joke?"

"Aye I do," Jay said, nodding his head. There was no doubt in his eyes. "It's a pretty intense joke, but a joke nonetheless. So you can wrap it up now guys – what, was this some kind of bachelor party joke in advance? Jesus. I almost took this seriously for a second there. Look at me – I'm fucking sweating man."

He was still grinning.

"Game's up guys. Bet you weren't expecting me to work it out so soon, eh?"

Davie and Iain exchanged bewildered looks. Iain left it up to Davie to do the talking.

"Jay…"

"Was Rachel in on it?" Jay asked. "Was she? Man, I nearly had a heart attack when I found her sprawled out in the garden like that. That shit's not funny guys. She's pregnant – what was I supposed to think?"

Davie's poker face remained intact.

"I've got nothing to do with this. I swear to God guys, I hope this *is* a joke but if it is then I'm not the clown."

Now it was Iain's turn to pick up the note. The handwriting *did* look feminine and that long, curved style was somehow familiar. "This doesn't feel like a joke."

Something about the way he said the words, dour and certain, brought Jay's delusion to a crashing halt.

Jay stared at them both. All the hope bleeding out of his eyes. "C'mon – are you both fucking around with me?"

Davie's stone-cold expression wasn't to be bargained with. "No."

"No?"

"Jay," he snapped, "we've been kidnapped. For real, no fucking joke. Who in their right mind would think this is a joke? I get it – you're in shock. You're in denial. Whatever. But this is real and you'd better accept it."

Jay's back fell against the wall. It looked like he was about to slide down to the floor, burst into tears. "Last time I'm going to ask," he said, his voice cracking. "And no fucking around, okay? I'm not in the mood. Is this a prank?"

His eyes begged for confirmation.

Iain shook his head.

"Swear to God man," Davie said. "It's no joke."

Jay charged across the kitchen and lashed out at the pantry door with the heel of his shoe. He kicked it repeatedly like he was fleeing a housefire and the door was the last obstacle in between him and safety. "Fuck. Fuck. Fuck."

Iain smiled. He couldn't help it.

When he was done bludgeoning the pantry door, Jay hurried over to the opposite wall, grabbed both ends of the tartan curtains and pulled them apart. Another barrage of morning light flooded the kitchen. Felt to Iain like someone had just shone a torch in his eyes.

"Anything interesting out there?" Davie asked.

Jay shielded his eyes with his hand. "Well, it's getting brighter."

"See anything else?"

"We're in the middle of nowhere," Jay said in a voice that sounded devoid of hope. "All I can see are white hills and nothing else for miles. It's still snowing."

"Do we even know if we're in Scotland?" Davie asked.

Jay pulled the curtains closed and turned to face the others. "It's a safe bet." He trudged away from the window, a dazed man walking to the guillotine. "Then again, we could be anywhere."

"There's water," Iain said, picking up a bottle off the table. "Food, whisky, electricity and heating." He walked over to the grimy, stainless-steel sink by the window and turned the tap. It made a dull squeaking noise but nothing came out.

"Bottled water it is," he said, lining up three glasses and pouring everyone a drink. "At least enough until..."

"Sunset," Davie said. "Enough until sunset."

"Aye."

Jay read the note again.

Iain watched, aware that the truth hadn't sunk in yet. Here was a man who, ordinarily at least, could cope with whatever life threw at him. A man who showed no weakness, and who'd acquired enough worldly experience to handle most situations with a certain finesse. Except today. Even though they hadn't seen each other in over twenty years, Iain recalled Jay's cool, *nothing's out of my control* exterior. Acting like he didn't give a shit. That's partly what made him such a good bully. Good bullies don't get hurt and if they do, they don't show it. But this wasn't school and they weren't fifteen anymore. Here in the cabin, Jay had lost control and now he had to be thinking about all the nice things he stood to lose if they didn't make it out alive. His woman. His job. His money – it was all slipping away and with each fresh reading of the note, it was only slipping away further.

What about Davie? Didn't he have a wife too? Kids? And yet he wasn't making a scene, not like Jay kicking in the pantry door. Davie remained still in his wheelchair, a crippled Zen monk, his eyes closed as he wrestled with the problem. Someone would miss him, Iain was sure of it. They'd miss Davie if he didn't come back.

Who would miss Iain? His family wouldn't notice his absence for months and even then, it'd probably be his landlord who contacted them to ask why Iain wasn't responding to emails or picking up the phone. What about Alison? They hadn't even kissed yet. They'd held hands briefly under the table one night in the pub. It was incredible. But would she even notice or really care if Iain just stopped showing up?

The thought of never seeing her again, of never feeling those butterflies as he drove up the A9, was terrifying.

"The reunion," Jay said, clicking his fingers as he sat down and slid the note back across the table. "It can't be a coincidence that the three of us were kidnapped on the eve of the Class of '95 reunion? Were any of you planning on going?"

Iain shook his head.

Davie did likewise. "Nope."

Jay jumped back to his feet now. Pacing the room, chewing on the tip of his finger as he concentrated.

"Holy shit, it's the reunion."

"What does that mean exactly?" Davie asked. He drank some water, following Jay's non-stop movement across the kitchen as he put the glass to his lips. Iain wondered if Davie was envious of people when he saw them walking. Like Jay was walking now. Or was that stupid?

"Are you seriously suggesting that someone from school has something to do with this? Someone from our old year?"

"Aye," Jay answered.

"What happened to Lenny Sanderson?"

"The people we went to school with," Iain said, butting in, "weren't exactly master criminals in the making. Most of them were posh kids from nice homes."

Jay wagged a finger in the air. "That doesn't mean shit."

"He's right," Davie said, looking at Iain. "We're not the same people we were. Why should they be?"

"And I was right about something else," Jay said, stopping dead and turning towards the kitchen window. "This *is* a prank. But it's not our prank. Someone outside is running the show."

"A prank?" Davie said, glancing at the note. "I was on a train in the north of England for God's sake. I wasn't in my house or at work. I was on a moving train. How did they know where I was?"

Jay scratched the tip of his chin. "It's not hard to track people down nowadays mate. Is it? Not if you're determined, not if you have a basic grasp of online stalking. Is Elena on Facebook?"

"All the time."

"Someone probably sent her a friend request. Weeks ago. Months ago, maybe. Poor woman thought it was harmless and accepted. Is she the sort of person who posts about everything she does? Everything she eats? Everywhere she goes."

Davie nodded. "Sounds like you know her."

"And if she writes about everything in her life," Jay said, "then she writes about you. Right?"

"I suppose so."

"Hey presto," Jay said. "That's a way in for the online stalker. That's how they knew you were coming up to Glasgow this weekend. You said the guy on the train had a photo of your house on his phone. I hate to say this Davie but they've probably been watching the house for weeks. Months. Who knows? These people, they're organised. And there seems to be quite a lot of them."

"People from school?" Davie said, looking like a man who'd just been told the sun was a green square. "Our old classmates? Stalked us? Assaulted us? Kidnapped us? That's crazy talk man."

"Davie," Jay said, emptying the glass of water in his hand. "What else could it be? They only knocked us out for a couple of hours. Big deal. They didn't inject us with heroin or turn us into addicts. And they're not going to murder us either, that's bullshit. It's a sick joke! The note, the threat, the killer thing – it's all made up to freak us out. They want to scare us. They want to get us back for what we did to them."

Davie glanced at Iain, far from convinced.

"Jay..."

But Jay was on a roll. "Think about it guys. They've got the legend here, right here in all three parts. They've got the Lads. And what could be more fun than pranking the Lads, than scaring the utter bejesus out of the Lads at the school reunion?"

Jay's eyes took on a sudden, intense focus. "That's what we are. We're a finale. We're a fucking main event."

He walked the kitchen perimeter at a dizzying speed, pointing to the ceiling and walls. "The proof's in here some-where." He traced his finger along the dusty edges towards the corners and back again. "I'll bet there's a hidden camera installed in every room."

Iain and Davie watched in silence. Jay was too busy searching for the damning evidence to notice the doubt on their faces.

He spun around. Held a finger up in the air.

"Didn't what's her name...Jill Clark...go on to make films for the BBC? Remember her? I heard she made a music video in 2002 or something like that. For someone famous – some pop star from a reality TV show. Remember Jill Clark? Tiny girl, chip on her shoulder the size of a house. Bit of a smart arse too."

"I think you're reaching," Davie said. "Jill Clark was a tiny wee specky girl, frightened of her own shadow."

Jay went back to probing the walls, searching for pinhole cameras. He worked at a maddening speed. "People grow up. People change. But the old resentments, they linger."

"She hated us," Iain said. "I remember that much."

Davie let out a harsh laugh. "A lot of people hated us. That doesn't mean they turned into the Count of Monte Cristo. Most people get over the shit they had to deal with in the school playground. They move on."

"Do they?" Iain asked.

Davie looked at Iain. "I don't know."

Jay walked back to the table. "Think about it boys. Why weren't we going to the reunion? Because we're not welcome, that's why. Can you imagine the three of us – the Lads – walking back into Strathmore tonight as if nothing ever happened? Hey Jay, good to see you again. Iain, Davie – hi! Thanks for making my life a living hell back in the day. Kinda hoped you'd all died a miserable death by now. Still, there's plenty of time yet."

"This is insane," Davie said. "I'm getting my phone and

calling the men in the white coats. There's a padded cell with your name on the door, Jay."

Jay's eyes lit up. "You have a phone?"

"Of course not," Davie said. "Anyway, I highly doubt we'd get a signal up here."

"It's a prank," Jay said. "It's a sick prank and I'll bet you a grand they're recording this for the reunion tonight. They're going to play it on a big screen and they're going to piss themselves laughing at us."

Iain looked up at the ceiling. He saw a network of cracks, yellow stains and other markings on the cornice. No cameras.

"Fuck it," he said. "I'm going outside."

Jay nodded. "Me too. If I'm right about this, then they're out there. At least, some of them are out there."

"I don't know," Davie said. "I don't know if that's a good idea."

But Jay was already following Iain to the kitchen door. He talked like he was making a public announcement. "We confront the bastards. Aye? I'm going to sue every single one of them when we get out of this fucking hut." He spun around, both thumbs up, searching for the secret cameras. "Great stuff guys." He clapped his hands together. "I'll see you in court."

Iain and Jay walked to the front door.

"Careful guys," Davie said, wheeling after them. He stopped at the edge of the hallway. "We don't know what's out there."

"I know exactly what's out there," Jay called back. "I kicked their arse back in the day and now I'm going to drag every single one of them through court for kidnapping, assault and every other charge I can think of."

Iain led the way. He turned the door handle, expecting

to find it locked. It wasn't, but it was freezing cold to touch. When he pulled the door open, a gust of freezing cold Arctic air blew inside the cabin.

"Shit," he said. "That's nasty cold."

Jay pinched the collar of his shirt closed. "We're not exactly dressed for this."

They walked outside. It was still early morning and there was a hint of leftover mist in the air. But the mist was fizzling out and overall, visibility was good. Iain heard the bright chirp of birdsong. Then a sudden flap of wings over-head as if they'd disturbed someone by coming outside. The air was fresh, deliciously so after the musty smell of the cabin.

Iain looked around. There was a small section of paved decking at the front of the cabin. A seating area? Whatever it was, whatever it had once been, it was gradually disap-pearing under the snow. Iain imagined how nice it would be to spend time here in the summer with Alison and his friends from Gairloch – his *real* friends. Some outdoors furniture. Drinks on the table, a heating lamp overhead and that gorgeous, unspoiled sky and the clear horizon. It wasn't hard to envision the cabin as a neat little holiday home. Sad to think that it had been neglected over the years.

"See anything?" Jay asked, using his hand as a visor.

Iain answered in a low voice. "Nope. Not yet."

"Shit, it's cold out here."

"I know."

Their shoes made a loud crunching noise on the snow. It wasn't a thick covering yet, but it was enough to add an extra touch of seasonal magic to the surroundings.

Where was the road? Where was anything?

Iain glanced at the cabin exterior. It wasn't much, possibly a converted byre that dated back to the nineteenth-century. Now it was a crumbling wreck, isolated and not another building in sight.

"I can't see anything," Jay said, his voice shivering along with the rest of him. "Grass, hills – is that it?"

"I think there's a loch up there too," Iain answered. He zipped his WH Smith fleece as far as the zipper went. All he had on was the fleece, a shirt, a pair of black trousers and shoes. Still, he was better off than Jay with his crumpled shirt minus the suit jacket. To Iain, Jay looked like a drunken yuppie trying to make his way home after an all-nighter at the wine bar.

"HELLO!"

Jay's voice echoed back from the hills.

Hello, hello, hello.

Iain stared at the horizon. The sky was a work of art – a beautiful shade of dark blue up top and pinkish orange underneath where the sun was still coming up. Indeed, the outline of a pear-shaped loch was barely visible underneath the emerging sunrise. It was at least a couple of miles away from the cabin's location. Probably more than that.

No electric lights. No roads. Nothing. It was like they'd been dropped at the far end of the world.

"What do we do?" he whispered. "What if there's no one here?"

Jay's usual confidence was absent in his voice. "I don't know. If we're on our own, then we need to keep going. Walk for a bit, aye? Go downhill and see if there's a clearer view. Maybe we'll find a road. There has to be something – hikers, for God's sake. Maybe...maybe this is the joke. What if they've abandoned us here with no money and no phones and now we have to get back to Glasgow by ourselves?"

Iain didn't like the thought of that.

"C'mon," Jay said. "Let's keep going."

He waited for Iain to lead the way.

They walked forward a few paces before stopping dead. There was a noise up ahead, something like footsteps in the snow. But it wasn't Iain or Davie making the sound.

"Did you hear that?" Iain asked.

A pause.

"Aye."

It came closer – the crunching of snow underfoot. About twenty metres up ahead, Iain noticed a dip in the land, a sudden slope leading downhill. The noise was coming from over there – it was someone walking uphill towards the cabin. Towards them.

"Iain," Jay whispered. "We need to get back to the c..."

"Shhh..."

Iain pressed a finger to his lips.

"See them?"

There was more than one of them. A cluster of shapes, maybe ten to fifteen in total appeared at the crest, shrouded in dawn mist. Iain saw only their vague outlines at first, but whoever it was, they were walking with purpose.

The group came to a halt. Iain still couldn't see them properly.

"Stop," a man's voice yelled. He sounded angry. "Where do you two think you're going?"

"Alright," Jay said, taking a step forward. He gave Iain a tap on the arm, as if signalling for Iain to follow. Iain stayed put. "Enough of this. We know who you are and why you're doing this. And quite frankly, it's ridiculous."

The reply was gruff and to the point. "Get back in the cabin."

Jay flashed his middle finger, holding it up high so everyone could see. "This isn't funny you guys. We're not at school anymore and I'm not amused. Now I'm warning you

– if you don't call off the joke, I'm going to start getting legal on your arse. Every last one of you."

The man at the front stepped ahead of the pack. There was something swinging at his side, hidden in the mist along with all the other detail. The others followed the speaker, albeit at a slower pace.

When they emerged from the mist, Iain's blood ran cold.

"Good God," Jay said, backing off. His retreat was so sudden that he almost lost his footing and tripped over.

The kidnappers were wearing masks. The masks had been crudely designed in the shape of a human face, one made of old leather and fabric. A collage of tiny white and pink feathers hung from the eye slits and a mop of reddish-brown hair, along with a straggly beard, complimented the ghastly human-like appearance. There were even wooden stumps in the mouth, acting as teeth.

"What do you want?" Jay asked, his voice cloaked in terror.

"Get back in the cabin," the leader said. His voice was a muffled growl through the mouthpiece. He lifted the rifle at his side. Now the barrel was up, pointing at the two men standing in front of the old cabin. "You've read the note, I take it?"

"Yes," Jay said. "We read it but..."

"Then do as instructed. Unless that is, the killer is ready to confess?"

"Confess to what?" Jay said, his voice cracking. "There's no killer in there. We're not murderers. This is bullshit and we know it's got something to do with Strathmore Academy, right? It's the reunion, aye? Show yourselves for God's sake – take those stupid masks off and put those toy guns away."

The masks were silent.

Somehow, Jay barked out a laugh. "Ah-ha! Didn't think

we'd figure it out so soon?" The cockiness crept back into his voice. "It's not exactly rocket science, is it? Seeing as how we've..."

The gunshot sounded like a whip cracking in Iain's ears. It came without warning and it reverberated through the hills with tremendous force. Iain staggered backwards, grabbing a stunned Jay by the arm and steering him back to the cabin.

"Jesus Christ!" Jay yelled. "Are you fucking crazy? Fucking shooting at us?"

"They're not toys," Iain said. "C'mon!"

He tightened his grip on Jay's arm, hauling him backwards at a dizzying speed. His feet floundered in the snowy conditions and Iain almost went down twice, taking Jay with him.

The two men clung to each other, bonded by fear.

"Before sunset!" the leader yelled.

Jay and Iain hurried back into the cabin. Once they were inside, Iain slammed the door shut, pressing his body against the wood. They were back – back in the box, surrounded by the smell of hay and damp rotting soil.

Davie's chair came tearing down the hallway.

"What happened?"

Jay didn't answer. He was too busy examining the door handle. "There's no key. No sliding bolt. Oh shit! We can't lock this fucking door from the inside. Fuck! Fuck! Fuck! They can come in any time they want."

He doubled over. Buried his head in his hands.

"Breath Jay," Davie said. "Take a deep breath. You too Iain."

Iain's back was up against the wall. He was reliving the encounter outside, particularly the moment where the masks had emerged through the mist. That had been worse than the unexpected shooting.

"What happened?" Davie asked for a second time.

"There's a whole pack of them out there," Jay said, straightening up. "About fifteen or something. They're wearing these creepy fucking masks. They've got guns too."

Davie's skin turned a sickly grey colour. "What did they say? About the school connection. Did you ask them about that?"

"They didn't say much," Iain said. "Follow the instructions, that's about it."

Davie cursed under his breath.

"Then what? They tried to shoot you?"

"It was a warning shot," Iain said. "If they wanted to shoot us, we'd be dead by now."

Jay's eyes were distant, like he was still out there in the snow. "They're going to kill us. I think...I think they're really going to kill us Davie."

Davie buried his face in his hands. "I thought it was a prank. You said it was a prank Jay – you were so convinced that..."

"This is *not* a prank," Iain said. "Let's just stop fucking saying that, eh?"

Jay mumbled something that Iain didn't understand. Then he hurried down the hallway and came back seconds later waving the note in his hand.

"Okay," he said. "Who's the killer?"

"Don't you fucking dare," Iain said. "Don't you dare look at me." He felt the blood rush to his face. His fingers curled into tight fists although he kept them lowered at his sides. "I told you already, I haven't killed anyone."

"Easy," Davie said, subtly manoeuvring his chair in

between the two men. "Take it easy guys. We'll figure this thing out, aye? It's going to be okay."

Iain backed away, took a deep breath. Jay's back was still up against the door, eyes staring blankly down the hallway.

"Those masks…"

6

———

DAVIE

"Lenny Sanderson," Jay said. "Well, that confirms it. It's Lenny Sanderson."

Davie groaned. "Back to Lenny now, are we?"

"Guns," Jay said, hitting one hand off the other for emphasis. "They've got fucking *guns*."

The men were back in the living room. The front door to the cabin was firmly shut but not locked, much to their horror. The living room door was closed too. Davie had been shocked at how much time and effort Jay and Iain had put into trying to secure both doors. Jay suggested they drag as much furniture out of the living room as they could, take it down the hallway, and barricade the entrance with it. Davie had to remind him that there was a back door too, that there were several windows scattered throughout the cabin. If the kidnappers really wanted to get in, he'd said, they'd find a way.

Davie sat in his chair, watching a frustrated Jay as he paced the room. Every now and then, Jay would march over to the window, peel back the curtains an inch and check if anyone was out there. Then he'd go back to walking, chewing the tips of his fingers. Talking to himself.

What had they seen in the snow? Davie had the others' description of the masks, of the shooting, of everything that happened outside, but he hadn't seen it for himself. Clearly, it made all the difference.

In contrast to Jay's constant motion, Iain sat on the couch in silence. Fingers interlocked on his lap.

"You don't know it's Lenny Sanderson for sure," Davie said.

Jay barked out a laugh. "Don't I?"

"There are other possible explanations, some of them we've already covered. In fact..."

Davie stopped. Leaned back slowly in his chair.

He wasn't ready to go there yet.

"In fact what?" Jay asked.

"Doesn't matter."

"It's Lenny Sanderson," Jay said, pointing to the window. "Davie, they're armed to the teeth out there. Why did my boss have to hire a crook for God's sake? Why did I have to be in a two-man promotion race against a fucking *villain*?"

"C'mon Jay," Davie said. "Did you see him out there? Did you recognise his voice?"

Jay turned to Davie, sweat running down his face. "How many villains do *you* know with a grudge?"

"Someone's got a grudge," Davie said with a nod. "But we don't know for sure who that is. Right now, we don't know anything. We're just tossing theories up in the hope that something sticks."

Jay brought his face closer to the window, which was speckled with snowflakes and water droplets.

"They're gone," he said.

He closed the curtains and turned back to the others. "Shit, if you hadn't been there with me Iain, I'd swear on the Bible that I'd imagined the whole thing. That was like a nightmare. Like something out of a horror film."

Iain nodded. "Aye."

"We're helpless," Jay said. "Completely fucking helpless."

Helpless.

There was that word. If there was one thing that Davie knew, it was the feeling of being helpless. That had been his experience of the world after getting out of hospital five years ago. His legs didn't work. He'd been told by the therapists to 'incorporate the wheelchair as a part of himself.' To accept it. But he couldn't. How was he supposed to get used to a body that didn't work the way it had worked for his entire life up to that point? His mobility, his independence, his self-image, all of it had been wiped out by that out-of-control lorry on Argyle Street.

Helpless.

After coming home from the hospital, discovering the house full of modifications – ramps, handrails, alterations to doorways and changes in the bathroom – instead of being grateful, Davie's resentment had skyrocketed. The only thing that made him feel better was the knowledge that he could end his life whenever he wanted. Pills. Slitting his wrists open. Cutting his throat. Those seemed like the most practical options. In the end, it was only the thought of Elena and the kids that stopped Davie from going through with it. Unable to bear the thought of what it would do to them, Davie stepped back from the precipice and tried to accept his new life. It was the hardest thing he'd ever done. There were no simple things anymore – getting from the house to the car, taking a shower, getting from the car to the shops – it was a brand-new world for the man with no legs.

He'd overcompensated at first, trying to do too much too fast. He recalled the first time he'd gone to the pub with a group of friends, a *normal* man resuming a *normal* life. Davie insisted that he didn't need any help when it was his round. So off he went, taking his chair up to the bar, determined to get it right. It was a disaster. After yelling out his order, he struggled to get his wallet out of his bag. Mostly, because he was trying to do things at the old speed. He hadn't adjusted yet. Even when he got the drinks, Davie almost spilled the tray on the way back to the table. Again, he was going too fast. Sweating by that point. Everyone was laughing at him, at least, that's how it felt to Davie. Or they felt sorry for him. Which was just as bad.

Acceptance came in the end, but slowly. It came through talking, even laughing about his situation, this new way of life that piece by piece, became a little less confusing over time. He didn't like it. He'd never like it. But Davie never forgot the names of the people who hadn't survived the lorry crash. Never forgot their faces. People who'd never kiss their kids goodnight again. Who'd never feel the sun on their face or enjoy a glass of wine with a loved one.

Helpless? Sure, the three men trapped inside the cabin were helpless. At least for now. In the meantime, they'd have to keep going. As Davie knew from experience, gritting it out was sometimes the best road that led to a solution.

"I saw him last night," Jay said. "No one believed me when I told them at dinner. I saw that bastard, Lenny Sanderson, standing on the main street, right around the corner from where I live. He's been watching me. Stalking me."

"Are you sure?" Davie asked. "That it was him?"

Jay nodded. "I am now."

Iain pushed himself off the couch. "I'm getting the whisky. Going for a piss too, as long as the toilet works. Anyone want anything? Food? Water?"

"Just bring the whisky," Jay said. "And three glasses."

Davie listened as Iain's heavy, plodding footsteps disappeared down the hallway. He could hear the wind too. Whistling. Hissing. Sounded like a giant kettle boiling outside the house.

"This guy," he said, turning to Jay. "This Lenny Sanderson you're talking about. He's your rival at work?"

"Aye," Jay said.

"How do you *know* he's dodgy?"

Jay lowered his voice, like a spy about to spill top secret information. "Charlie Peacock, a guy in accounts, he took me aside one morning and tried to warn me off running against Sanderson for the CFO job. I thought he was crazy. Not your time Jay, he said. Let this one pass. Later on, he told me he'd been out for a few beers with Sanderson one night after work. It turned into a full-on drinking session. Whisky. Shots – the lot. Sanderson got pissed out his skull, started boasting about being in prison for armed robbery. He told Charlie about the things he'd done to the guy who slept with his wife."

Davie shrugged. "Maybe it's just all talk."

"You don't know this guy Davie. There's something off about him. Something very *wrong*."

"How the hell was a guy like that working for your company in the first place?" Davie asked.

Jay shook his head. "I've asked myself that question a thousand times. My guess? There's a family connection in the company or something like that. Either that or he's got compromising photos of one of the higher ups and he bribed his way in. Who knows?"

"Still sounds pretty thin man. And there's one glaring question we've overlooked."

"What?"

"Why would Lenny Sanderson kidnap me?" Davie asked. "And why would he kidnap Iain? This grudge between the two of you, what's it got to do with us?"

"You're not seeing the big picture, Davie."

"Enlighten me."

"He's a clever bastard," Jay said. "He's done his research on me, biding his time and he's worked out that the best way of getting away with this is if he puts the spotlight on someone else. Or on a group of people for that matter."

Davie shrugged. "I don't follow."

"The grudge," Jay said. "He wants to make it look like it's someone else's grudge that got me kidnapped. So, Lenny's doing his research. Or he's got someone else doing his research for him. They find out about the Lads. About Strathmore, about the reunion tonight. He knows this is the perfect time to strike and with you and Iain here, well it points the finger in the other direction, eh? Back to school."

"That still sounds like the more plausible theory," Davie said. "And what about the note? How does that fit into your theory?"

Jay shrugged. He was picking at the upholstery on the couch again. "I don't know. Metaphor, fuck knows. I sure as hell killed his career at Global, that's for sure."

They listened to the sound of the toilet flushing.

Jay was calm now, in stark contrast to his earlier pacing. "I've got a fiancée and a kid on the way. I need to get back home."

He walked over to the curtains again, peered through

the gap and squinted at the daylight. To Davie's surprise, Jay reached for the dusty window handle. He watched as Jay wrestled it loose, then pushed the window open a few inches.

Davie flinched at the cold breeze seeping into the cabin. It knocked the air out of his lungs. "Jay. What are you doing?"

But Jay didn't respond. Instead, he leaned into the narrow gap he'd opened up and cupped his hands over his mouth. "Lenny Sanderson! Is that you? Are you out there?"

Nothing but the wind.

"Lenny! C'mon man, let's talk about this. If you're out there..."

Iain thundered back into the living room with the whisky bottle tucked under his arm. In one hand, he carried three glasses with the assurance of a waiter. "Are you trying to talk to them or something?"

"Don't ask," Davie said. "We're still on the Lenny Sanderson theory in here."

"I just saw one of them at the kitchen window," Iain said, putting the glasses down on the wobbly coffee table. The table swayed to one side under the weight and Iain pushed it back into place.

"What?" Davie asked.

"One of the masks. Leathery face with eyeslits, hair, beard, wooden teeth – the whole shebang. At the window, just there when I grabbed the whisky."

"That's perfect," Jay said, slamming the front window shut and pulling the curtains over. He turned back to the others. "They're watching all sides of the house then, eh? Making sure we don't make a run for it."

"Fat chance of that," Davie said.

Jay glanced at the wheelchair. "I didn't mean..."

"I know."

The room was silent for a moment.

"Masks," Davie said, tapping a finger off the edge of the table. "Why are they wearing masks?"

Jay spoke without a trace of humour in his voice. "And they used to call you the clever one? Why are they wearing masks? Because they want to hide their faces of course."

Davie nodded. "Aye right, smart arse. Well, there goes your Lenny Sanderson theory down the toilet."

"Eh?"

"Think about it. If Sanderson hired heavies to bump us off up here in the arse end of nowhere, what does he care if we see their faces or not? You don't need a mask if you're going to kill someone."

"Maybe he just wants to scare me," Jay said. "Who knows if he actually intends to kill us or not? I'm not a fucking mind reader, am I?"

Davie jerked a thumb towards the window. "He went to all *this* trouble just to scare you? No chance. There's a lot easier ways to scare someone Jay."

There was a look of fixed concentration on Davie's face.

"They're wearing masks because they don't want us to recognise them. You understand? They don't want us to *recognise* them. Which means that if we saw them unmasked, we'd know their faces."

"Who's out there?" Iain said. "Who's doing this to us?"

Davie looked at Iain with a sober expression. "Our old classmates. It's them – it *has* to be them."

Jay doubled over. It looked like he was about to throw up or pass out. "I just want some answers. This is criminal behaviour for God's sake, do they really think they're going to get away with this? Kidnapping? Threats of murder?"

Iain poured out three glasses of whiskey. He handed them out, then glanced at Davie.

"Why? Why are they doing this?"

Davie stared across the room. Thousands of dust particles floated in the narrow chink of daylight in between the curtains.

"It's *not* a prank. Someone's got a hell of a grudge against the three of us. Against the Lads. We must have pissed someone off more than we thought. Because this thing, it took a whole lot of planning. Took a whole lot of balls."

"Any ideas?" Jay said, lifting his hands off his face. He looked bleary-eyed and exhausted. "Who would do this to us?"

Davie reached for the whisky. "It's a big list," he said. "Take your pick."

JAY

You have it coming Jay. And you know why?

Because you had so much fun back then, didn't you?

How easy it was. Being a king. Being a king with Davie who, if you really admit it, ran the show better than you ever could, and with Iain who had Mike Tyson's shoulders and a face that only a mother could love.

You? You were big and you looked good. Walking around the school corridor with a look that said 'kill' and yet you were just an insecure teenager, full of fear, just like the rest of them.

You guys ruled that class of '95 though. Back when it was important to project strength amongst one's peers. Back when appearance and reputation were everything. School days – the happiest days of your life, so they say. When every little glance across the corridor is full of meaning, when every little imperfection is scrutinised, and when one false step can ruin everything.

School.

Where you were a king.

Why? Why did you love hurting the other kids so much? Yes, you did. You loved it ya lying prick. Fucking sociopathic devil that you are. What was lacking in the teenage Jay Green at the time that meant flushing Ronnie Jarvis's head down the toilet – a piss-filled toilet – made you laugh so much? Fucking sadistic man. He was a wee speccy guy, harmless and pudgy, and yet you didn't fail to get in his face every time he had the misfortune to bump into you in the corridor.

Imagine being him. How do you think he felt, leaving the house for school every day? Knowing that you were in there. Waiting.

What was missing? What's still missing?

No one liked you Jay. You know that, don't you? People smiled and laughed at your jokes but not because they liked you or thought you were funny. It was because they were scared and they thought if they did what you wanted then you and your sadistic mates would leave them alone.

Is it any surprise that this has happened? That someone wants you to suffer?

Wants you to die.

Jay, you have it coming.

————

Jay didn't even like whisky that much. But he drained that first glass, hoping that Mr Johnnie Walker Black Label would work his magic and mute the train of thought reminding Jay about every single shitty thing he'd ever done. Even though he *had* to think about it because how else were they going to come up with a suspect?

He took a second glass.

God, Jay found himself envying Iain. Iain didn't have the likes of a Rachel to worry about. He didn't have a baby on the way that needed a father. Jay couldn't stop imagining his pregnant fiancée lying in the back garden in Glasgow, exposed to the elements. In his mind's eye, he saw the masks standing over her, those awful, withered masks that looked like the skin of a long-dead corpse, peeled off and wrapped around someone's face.

Don't crack, he told himself. Don't you dare crack.

Jay and Iain were back on the same couches they'd woken up on earlier that day. Hours had passed since they'd first woken up, but how many? The clock on the wall was broken and their phones were gone. Jay had taken his Rolex off before going into the bathroom last night and neither Davie or Iain wore a watch. Three hours? Four hours? Was it more? There'd been long periods of silence in the cabin living room, punctuated by frenzied bouts of speculation about the identity of their kidnappers. No one touched the food. Only a little water and of course, the whisky consumption was the best nourishment available to them.

Davie's wheelchair, parked at the edge of the coffee table, gave him the best view of the main window. He rarely took his eyes off it.

You haven't seen the masks yet, Jay thought. He didn't envy Davie for still having that to look forward to.

"Alright," Jay said, rubbing his hands together to generate warmth. It was getting increasingly cold in the cabin despite the electric heaters turned up full. "Where are we with this thing?"

Iain picked up the bottle, poured a few drops of whisky into his glass. "Still in deep shit."

"I get that," Jay said. He inhaled the peaty scent coming from his own glass and took a sip. "What else have we got?"

"The stickiest theory we have," Davie said, taking his eyes off the window, "is the school connection. It keeps coming back to that. That one person, obviously with some help, is responsible for all of this. This person is motivated by revenge. They're holding a massive grudge against the Lads – against us. This person is clearly unhinged. Does anyone know who organised the reunion tonight?"

Jay shrugged. "Not really. Most of it was organised on Facebook – there's a few names attached that are involved in the admin side. Nicola Hamilton. Jane Stevenson. All the old prefects, eh? The mumsy types. I don't think they're the kidnapping type though, do you?"

"No," Davie said. "I doubt it."

"Anyway," Jay continued, "we're not the Lads anymore. If someone's holding a grudge against the Lads then it's a waste of time. We're different people. I'm Jay, you're Davie and Iain's Iain. The Lads have been gone for twenty years. Chase the Lads, you're chasing ghosts."

Davie nodded. "I agree. Now, go tell that to whoever's out there with the massive grudge."

Jay let out a loud sigh. He put his glass down on the table, leaned back and crossed his legs. Looked to Davie like he was about to conduct a job interview.

"Tonight," he said, "in Glasgow, our school reunion will take place. Can't be coincidence, right? We're not going so someone wants a private reunion up here. And they want to wear scary masks, even though Halloween's already been this year. And they want us to freak out because they've lied to us, telling us that there's a killer amongst us."

"And if there is a killer," Iain said. "Then there's a liar too."

The living room fell silent.

Davie ingested some of that musty odour that lingered inside the cabin. "We don't know it's just a game. We don't know it's just a mindfuck either. I don't think they're doing this to scare us – it's about justice. It's payback."

Jay ran his fingers through his hair. "Payback? C'mon. We were kids and we didn't know any better."

"We were vicious bastards," Davie said. "And for the record, we *were* old enough to know better."

Jay grabbed the bottle. Another top up, but at least the hangover and the dull ache in his ribs were gone. Hallelujah.

"Take it easy you two," Davie said. He was pointing at the whisky bottle, which was getting lighter in a hurry. "We need clear heads and you're both putting the whisky away like it's happy hour."

"C'mon Davie," Jay said. "My nerves are in tatters man. Someone took a shot at me today, eh? With a fucking rifle."

Davie's blank expression didn't change.

"Back to the matter at hand."

"Yes," Jay snapped. "The matter at hand. Okay, we were bullies. We were vicious wee bastards who didn't care what we did or who we hurt. Alright? It happens boys, it happens. It happens in every school in every country around the world and it always will because that's just the way it is with kids, with teenagers at that awkward stage of life. There's a pecking order. There's a group of alpha kids who take it too far. And just to be clear, not all bullies get kidnapped twenty-five years later. Most people just get on with life."

The living room descended into an eerie silence. There was only the sound of the wind and an occasional clicking noise from the heaters.

"Jay," Davie said.

"What?"

"We did a lot more than call people names. A *lot* more." He drained his glass in one fell swoop and winced as the alcohol burned his throat. Felt pretty good though. "It keeps me awake at night, even now. All these years later."

"What?" Jay asked.

"The things we did back then."

"Me too," Iain said, staring into his glass with the famous Lewis dead-eyes. It was like he was hundreds of miles away and still in the same room. "It seems fitting that my life's a pile of shit, you know?"

Davie glanced at Iain. "You know, I *was* thinking about going to the reunion."

"What for?" Jay asked, barking out a laugh. "To apologise? To hand out chocolates, gift vouchers and hope that made everything okay?"

"Maybe."

"That's lunacy."

Iain sat up, inched forward on the couch. "You *do* remember, don't you Jay?"

"Remember what?"

"All the things we did."

"I don't think about it that much, Iain. And I sleep just fine at night for the record."

"Crashing house parties every weekend," Iain continued, "none of which we were invited to. Stealing beer and trashing other people's property just so they'd get in trouble with their folks. Forcing people to hand money over, telling them it was a loan and never paying back. Knowing that they'd never ask for it. And..."

He hesitated. Took another sip before continuing.

"...forcing girls to go upstairs with us, making them do things it was obvious they didn't want to do. That was us, all of us. And remember Kenny Mills? The first black kid in our year, showed up at the start of second year. Remember? How we forced him to show his dick to the entire maths class so we could find out if it was true what they said about black guys. Remember all this Jay?"

Jay glared at Iain over the rim of his glass. Said nothing.

Iain smiled. "Aye, I know you do. And that's just the tip of the iceberg."

"Ancient history," Jay said.

Looked like he was going to have to be the strong one. The other two were wallowing in self-pity and that would get them nowhere. Not when their lives were on the line. "Look, we're not killers. We *were* arseholes – we were cruel, despicable little pricks but we didn't kill anyone. And we don't deserve what's happening. Right?"

It was a long time before anybody spoke.

"Don't we?"

It was Davie.

"No we don't." Jay said.

Davie was back to staring at the window with that haunted look on his face. "What about...?"

"What?"

"What about Michelle Carson?" Davie said, turning to Jay. "Didn't you hear what happened to her?"

8

JAY

Jay's face was tight with concentration.

"Michelle Carson? Hmmm, I remember the name. What happened to her?"

Davie's tone of voice was sombre. "Blonde girl. She was so quiet – I hardly ever heard her speak. She was in maths with you Iain. Same chemistry class as us, Jay. Mrs Nimmo's class, remember?"

"Mrs Nimmo," Iain said, laughing softly. "God man, there's a blast from the past. The dragon lady."

Jay closed his eyes. Tried to reconstruct Michelle Carson's face in his head but although he recalled a vague outline, her features were lost to him. Maybe it was the weird bird noises coming from outside that distracted him. Hooting sounds, like someone mimicking an owl. Or maybe it was a real owl. What did Jay know about owls or birdsong or life in the sticks? He was out of his element here. A city boy trapped in a country nightmare.

He glanced at the others. No one else had said anything about the owl. Jay hoped to God he wasn't imagining it.

And there were other noises. Every now and then, Jay was certain he could hear creaking footsteps outside the cabin. A pair of boots trampling over fresh snow. Right outside – just behind that wall, metres away from the three men. Jay had no desire to get up and investigate. If it was *them*, it was a statement. It was their way of letting the three men inside the cabin know they were surrounded. Just a little reminder, not that Jay needed one. The whisky was good but it hadn't dulled the memory of those withered, leathery masks. And the thought of them just behind the curtain over there...

Confess.

"Do you remember her?" Davie asked.

Jay sat forward. "All I remember is she was a big girl. Blonde, bob-style haircut. Kind of plain looking, eh?"

"She wasn't that big," Davie said, shaking his head. "We called her fat but she was never fat. I remember the..."

He slammed his fist down on the arm of the chair.

Jay flinched. Looked at Iain, then Davie. Wondered if he'd missed something. "What is it mate?"

"I remember the scratches on her arms," Davie said, his voice cracking. He cleared his throat. Got it back together before continuing. "She always had scratches on her arms. I didn't understand what those were until years later. What she was doing to herself."

Iain nodded. "Didn't you put a bowl of ice cream on her desk once?"

"Yes," Davie said, staring up at the cobweb in the corner of the ceiling. "And if there's any justice, I'll burn in Hell."

Jay groaned and fell back onto the couch. This little trip down memory lane was getting them nowhere. They had a problem to solve, something immediate and urgent and they didn't have time to lament all the shitty things they'd done as teenagers. "Okay, we're scumbags. *Were* scumbags, a very long time ago. I'll ask again – how does that make us killers?"

"Didn't you hear?" Davie asked.

Jay hesitated. "Hear what?"

"Michelle Carson jumped off the Erskine Bridge about ten years ago."

There was a sudden tightening sensation in Jay's guts.

"Oh God."

"Aye."

"That rings a bell," Iain said, sitting forward on the other couch. Jay noticed he was slurring his words already. Made a mental note to keep tabs on how much Iain was drinking. "I do remember reading something about that on one of those old websites from the noughties, Friends Reunited or whatever it was called. There was a thread about her suicide and someone wrote that it was her mum dying of cancer that pushed her over the edge."

Jay glanced in Davie's direction. Gave a casual shrug of the shoulders. "See. It had nothing to do with us."

"Tell that to her brother," Davie said.

"What?"

"Her brother. He seems to think we're responsible."

"Oh Jesus," Jay said, standing up. It was so ridiculous he almost laughed out loud. "Are you shitting me? That big blond fucker. What was his name again?"

"Grant Carson."

"Shit," Iain said. "He *was* a big fucker. Mean as a snake too."

Jay picked up his glass and drank what was left. "I remember Carson. You know, I always wondered how a hulking psycho like that could have such a wallflower for a sister? Wait...what do you mean, *tell that to her brother*? Are you saying it's Grant Carson out there? *Grant Carson?*"

"I don't know," Davie said. "I saw him once, about two years after Michelle died. We bumped into one another in Tesco in Sauchiehall Street."

Jay frowned. "Okay. What happened?"

"We saw each other in the bread aisle. Our eyes met, it was awkward and without saying anything, I tried to walk past him. He blocked my exit. I tried again, he blocked me again. Then I just started blabbering on – told him I was sorry to hear about Michelle. I was talking shite pretty much. That made it worse. He leaned in. His eyes were blazing. Told me I might as well have pushed her off that bridge myself. Told me if he'd known how serious the bullying was back in school, that he would've killed all three of us."

Davie gestured for the whisky bottle. Iain topped up his glass.

"He said it wasn't over," Davie said, after a hasty sip. "That he'd never forget and that the three of us would never be safe."

"Perfect," Jay said. "He always was a charmer, the big man."

Davie's smile was grim. "I thought he was going to beat the shit out of me. Right there in the bread aisle of all places. But after saying that, he just walked away. I had the feeling it wasn't over."

"So," Jay said. "It was what – eight years ago? Surely if he was going to do something, he'd have done it by now. The sting of what happened to his sister, the loss, it's probably worn off."

"Or maybe he's been waiting."

"Grant Carson never struck me as the patient type," Iain

said. "More like a hothead who would've done something right away. In fact, he's probably a smackhead by now, eh? Wasn't he dealing coke for Terry Braithwaite and that other mad junkie that died, the one who hung around with Terry – ah fuck, what was his name again?"

"Beano," Jay said.

"Beano, aye. That was the guy who OD'd in Terry's house. Terry dumped him at the side of the road instead of calling for an ambulance."

Jay took a sip of whisky. "I remember that."

"Well, that's the sort of people we're talking about here," Iain said. "Junkies. Wasters, the lot of them. Grant Carson's dead or in prison by now."

"No," Davie said in a quiet voice. "Grant was a dealer, not a user. He's smarter than you think and if you ask me, he knows some very unpleasant people who'd be only too willing to help out with a triple kidnapping. Point is – we're looking for a someone with a major grudge against us. There you go."

"And it ties in with the school theory," Jay said.

"Aye," Davie said. "It..."

He was cut off by a loud cracking noise from inside the cabin. Jay's heart almost stopped. He spun around to face the door. To him, it sounded like floorboards groaning under the weight of someone's feet. Who knows? The cabin was old and it was making all kinds of noises, especially with that wind blowing outside. But that one? The others heard it too because the living room fell silent.

"What was that?" Jay whispered.

Iain's lips moved slowly.

"Is there...?"

"Someone else is in the cabin," Davie said, staring at the living room door as if waiting for the handle to turn.

"No," Jay said. "It's just the wind."

Iain pointed to the door. "You think? Go check then."

"Fine, I will."

Jay stood up, took a swig of whisky straight from the bottle. He walked over and gripped the door handle. The cabin cracked under his weight, a series of miniature explosions in the floor and walls that accompanied every step.

"It's just the wind. You've heard this place – it creaks if you so much as breathe."

"Why are you still whispering?" Davie asked.

Jay didn't answer. Now he was imagining one of the masks in the cabin, a lone figure, slowly making their way down the hallway towards the living room. Blank eyes, feathered eye slits and wooden teeth.

Are you ready to confess?

"Keep talking," he said to the others. "Talk about anything – don't let the place go suddenly quiet."

He realised his arms were shaking, all the way up to the shoulders. Even now, forty-four years old, the new CFO at Global, a husband and father-to-be, Jay was still acutely aware of the old accusations. The accusations from school that he was nothing but a poser. Davie was the brains. Iain was the muscle and Jay, well he was kind of pretty. No substance though. An empty vessel. Davie and Iain, they were the real deal, especially when it came to shit getting done. Jay was the gutless himbo for the girls to drool over.

We'll see about that, he thought.

He walked into the hallway and shivered at the biting cold. He heard Iain and Davie talking behind him – something about Davie's work in IT. Jay hit the switch on the wall. The light flickered for about five seconds, making little difference when it finally came on. Most of the light in the hall was natural, pouring in through the small window beside the front door. Jay wondered how the kidnappers were even getting electricity into the cabin in the first place. There had to be some kind of generator, something designed for off-grid shacks like this one.

"Shit," he whispered, cursing himself for volunteering. Felt like he was watching himself in a horror movie. The unsuspecting victim, approaching certain death.

Stupid always dies first.

The cabin was quiet, except for the noise that Jay's feet were making on the floor. He crept along the hallway, opening the doors, always expecting one of the masks to jump out and wrap their hands around his throat. *Confess!* There weren't many rooms to check – it wasn't exactly an oversized, luxury Airbnb they were trapped in. Just the two bedrooms, the kitchen and a storage cupboard. Jay peered inside all of them, hitting the light and tensing up each time. He was ready to bolt if something leapt out at him.

But the bedrooms were empty. So was the kitchen and storage cupboard.

Jay noticed a few damp patches on the kitchen floor. Melted snow? Might have come off his or Iain's shoes after they'd been outside that one time. Jay was happy to settle with that explanation and move on. After checking the bedrooms for a second time, he decided that there was no one else in the cabin. It was just the old place creaking and groaning that had freaked them out.

He'd done his duty. Now it was time to go back to the living room and report.

He walked out of the bedroom, glanced to his right.

There was someone standing at the door.

Jay's body seized up in a rush of terror, limbs trembling. He observed the silhouette of a small person, framed in the doorway. The intruder stood still, arms loose at the sides.

There was a mask over the face, that straggly orange hair and the matching beard.

"Oh Jesus."

The shape moved towards him. *Floated* towards Jay.

There was no longer a mask. Jay was looking at a young woman with blonde hair. She was slightly overweight with short pudgy arms, dressed in a school blazer and skirt that boasted the green and black colours of Strathmore Academy. White skin. Plain, colourless features. Eyes that didn't blink.

"Michelle? Is that you?"

Outside, the wind howled and Michelle Carson floated down the hallway. Her bare feet were off the floor, lifeless blue eyes looking through Jay. Her arms were extended towards him, porcelain fingers curved as she reached for Jay's neck. Jay closed his eyes, too scared to move. He waited for the end, if this was indeed the end.

There was a high-pitched scream, the sound of someone falling from a great height.

And then, nothing.

Jay opened his eyes. He was alone.

"Jay?"

It was Davie, calling from the living room. "You alright?"

They didn't hear the scream, Jay thought. Her scream. Didn't hear any of it because it didn't happen. It *didn't* happen.

"Fine," Jay blurted out. Sounded like his voice was breaking all over again. "I'm fine." He felt the sweat clinging to his shirt. "I'll be there in a second."

His fingers trembled on the nearest door handle. Jay pushed the door open and almost fell into the gloomy bedroom, the larger of the two inside the cabin. He turned on the light, placing his back against the door.

Didn't happen.

Jay was shaking. He couldn't let the others see him like this.

Michelle Carson had been dead ten years. Ten years dead and what just happened a minute ago was because of Davie, fucking sad story Davie, filling his head with nonsense about a girl who'd most likely been doomed from the start. Facts, just the facts. Some people weren't tough enough to cope with the harsh realities of human existence. That's life. No point in passing on those weak genes to the next generation.

"Rest in peace," he whispered. "But stay the fuck away from me you dead bitch. I'm *not* responsible."

What he'd give to hold Rachel again. To hold his baby growing inside her and squeeze them both tight and never let go. Jay was a smart guy. He knew he had it good but he didn't know quite how good until faced with the prospect of never seeing them again.

He *had* to get home.

This place, this cabin – it was driving him crazy.

Had Rachel informed his parents that he was missing yet? What state of mind was she in? God, she must be so worried. Was she still hoping anxiously that Jay would return to the house with coffee and croissants in a paper bag from St. Louis, their local café? It was a Saturday so Jay wasn't due at work. But it was long past breakfast and lunchtime by now, right? Maybe Rachel thought he'd gone to the gym. To the tanning salon.

Without telling her?

Fuck. He didn't know anything.

How long before someone down there realised that something was wrong? Before they raised the alarm?

Breathe, breathe, breathe. He was trapped in the cabin, not only with Davie and Iain, but with the memories. Now all the ghosts that he'd buried were scratching at the soil. Resurrecting, reminding Jay of what he'd once been. Did he even deserve to get away and go back to his nice life in the city? He had no excuses. None apart from youth.

You're a monster, he told himself. You're a monster trying to hide behind the guise of a respectable, middle-class businessman. But it won't work. No amount of personal reconstruction, altering of narratives, no promotion, no tanning salon or fat wad of money in the bank, will ever change what you are.

"Enough," Jay said, taking his back off the door. He turned around, killed the light, and reached for the handle. "Enough self-pity, you stupid fucker."

He had to keep his shit together. He was the one holding the guys together and if Jay broke, everyone would break.

"All clear," he yelled to the others. "There's no one in here. See, I told you."

9

DAVIE

After Jay had given the all clear, Davie and Iain sat in silence in the living room.

They'd exhausted all feeble attempts at conversation. Small talk, the meaningful stuff – it wasn't happening. Now Davie sat in his chair, stealing the occasional glance at Iain, who was drinking Johnnie Walker's whisky like it was cold lemonade on a hot summer's afternoon.

Davie wanted to talk to Iain. He wanted to ask him about other things. Things that had nothing to do with work but about life in general and what that looked like for Iain today. Davie wanted to apologise. He knew that both he and Jay had distanced themselves from Iain after leaving school. It was abandonment and it wasn't fair. It didn't help that Iain had always been a bit on the strange side and Davie, perhaps trying to justify the desertion, told himself he'd needed a break.

He wanted to apologise but he didn't. Showing emotion,

that sort of thing had never come easy to Davie. He hadn't even cried at his dad's funeral.

In the end, Davie and Jay had drifted apart after school too. That was fine with Davie. He was only too keen to put the history of the Lads behind him and move on with the next chapter of his life, which had been college and saving up money to go travelling overseas for a while. In the following years, he'd heard snippets of information here and there about what Jay and Iain were doing. Mostly about Jay and how he'd gotten involved in petty drug-dealing for Terry Braithwaite. Then finally, Jay had sorted himself out and gone to college. Iain, he hadn't heard much about. Iain had kind of disappeared.

It was done.

The Lads were dead and buried.

And yet here they were, back together again. It was clear that someone else out there hadn't forgot about the Lads.

Jay walked back into the living room, closing the door behind him. He fell onto the couch, grabbed the whisky glass. "It's just the cabin making noises."

"You alright?" Davie asked. "You look a bit green around the gills."

Jay pointed to the window. "Can you blame me? We're at the mercy of maniacs. I don't suppose anyone here's ready to confess yet?"

"Don't start that shit again," Iain said. He slurred both *start* and *shit*. "I'm warning you Jay..."

Davie's ears pricked up. There was a sudden growling noise from outside and it cut Iain off in mid-threat.

"Do you guys hear that?" Davie asked.

Jay was on his feet, hurrying over to the window. He was about to peel back the curtains when he stopped. "That sounds like a car to me. Or a van or something – maybe it's one of the vans that brought us here? I knew there had to be a road somewhere. How far away do you think it is?"

"Not that far."

Davie brought the chair over to the window. Iain remained on the couch, clutching the glass of whisky.

"It's getting louder," Jay said, glancing at Davie. There was hope in the man's eyes and he wanted Davie to fuel that hope by saying the right things. "It's a car, isn't it? Sounds like a car. You think it's coming here?"

Davie nodded. "Could be, aye."

The two men fell silent. They stayed by the window, listening to a sudden, skidding noise in the distance. Squealing brakes. Doors thrown open. And then from afar, people were shouting – a frantic chorus of voices, all yelling at one another. The road, wherever it was, wasn't far.

"STOP!" a man's voice yelled. "Police!"

Davie flinched at the crack of gunshots. They sounded like cannon fire in his ears.

"Holy shit!"

Jay slid down to the floor, back pressed up against the wall. His voice was giddy with excitement. "Fucking hell! Davie, it's the police. Do you think…?"

"I think we should open the curtains," Davie said, steering the chair to the window. "Pull the window open, Jay. Let them know we're here."

Jay's head went from side to side like he was trying to shake a wasp out of his hair. "You want to get shot through the window? We do nothing – not until the shooting's over."

"We need to let them know we're here."

"Take my advice mate," Jay said. "Just for once, eh? Back that chair up, keep your head down and wait it out. Iain, you too – stay on the couch and drink. We wait till it's over and then we let them know we're here."

Davie sighed, but he saw the sense in Jay's thinking. Patience, he had to play it smart. With his heart thumping, he reversed the wheelchair back about a metre, keeping his eyes glued to the window. The skirmish outside was in full-flow.

"POLICE! POLICE – Stop right there, hands up or…"

More gunshots down on the road. It was louder now so maybe they were on the hill leading up to the cabin. *Bang-bang-bang.* So many loud pops in quick succession that is sounded like a fireworks display speeded up. Voices, yelling, then dropping down in volume. Gunshots. Screaming.

"POLICE. Drop your…"

"Run…!"

To Davie's surprise, there was a big shit-eating grin on Jay's face. As he looked at the others from the floor, both thumbs were up in the air.

"They've found us," he said. "We're going home boys, we're going home."

10

DAVIE

Even if this is it. Even if it's over and you're going home, you still owe it to the others to tell them what you did.

No?

Yes.

Because you might be the cause of all of this.

You don't really believe that it's Michelle Carson's big brother out there, do you? You never did, not deep down. That big psycho, getting revenge for the death of his sister all these years later? You sure you're not overplaying that encounter in the supermarket? Sure, it was tense but it wasn't that bad. Congrats though, you made it sound credible to Jay and Iain. Looks like Jay might have bought it.

But you know better, don't you? You know who's out there, why they're out there, and who it is they want a confession from.

The others have a right to know because they've been through hell and it's all your fault. You should have told them by now.

Davie boy.

Because of what you did that day. The day of the Argyle Street lorry crash. That's why you're here.

This is on you.

Tell them what you did.

Confess.

11

IAIN

The shooting didn't last long. Maybe a few minutes in total, between the arrival of the police and the fighting down on the roadside. But to the three men waiting inside the cabin for news, it felt like hours.

Iain hadn't left the couch. He'd listened to the gunfight with a strange sense of detachment. This was in contrast to Davie and Jay, who were almost pissing themselves with excitement over by the window. But to Iain, the shootout was no more thrilling than it would've been had he heard it coming off a TV in another room.

He looked over at his old friends, cowering by the window. *Friends*. He needed to stop thinking of them like that. They were nothing to him now. They'd aged well though, not that he'd ever tell them to their face. Sure, Davie was still scrawny and gaunt. But he could still pass for an indie rock star from the nineties. He was still the legend, *Davie fucking Muir*. And Jay was sporting the ageing male model look well, no surprises there. Bland perfection. Still a walking talking Ken doll. And yet Iain would have given his right arm for some of that bland perfection because women went crazy for it. He could just imagine all the horny bitches trying to catch Jay's eye in the pub. All the slags. Uncrossing their fake-tanned legs, wafting their perfume in his direction as they walked past.

Iain glared at them both. Even after all these years, he still felt painfully inadequate in their presence.

He was aware that he'd gained the most weight. He hadn't ballooned to obesity but where there had once been a solid slab of natural muscle, there was now a sad pudginess. He felt heavier. Slower. He was terrified about Alison seeing him naked for the first time. Would she run a mile when he took his shirt off? And what sort of lover would he be after all this time out of the game? It was a terrifying thought. Iain would have to be blind drunk when the big day came. Drunk and full of Viagra.

You've had too much whisky, he thought.

"How did the police find us anyway?" Davie asked, keeping his voice down as if someone might be listening on the other side of the window.

"Maybe someone saw us arrive," Jay said. He was still wearing that big dumb grin on his face. The colour was back in his cheeks. "Three vans, unloading three unconscious people from the back and taking them into a rundown old cabin. That's going to look suspicious to anyone, isn't it?"

The discussion was interrupted by a knock on the door. Jay and Iain stood up while Davie spun his chair around to face the hall. There was a second knock, followed by a gruff male voice.

"Police. Is there anyone in there?"

Jay answered before the man had even stopped talking. "Yes. Yes there is! Three people in here officer. My name's Jay

Green and I'm here with Iain Lewis and Davie Muir. Those people out there kidnapped us yesterday – they grabbed two of us in Glasgow and one of us off a train in the north of England."

There was a long pause.

"Is anyone hurt?"

"No," Jay called out. "A couple of bumps and bruises perhaps. A bit shaken up but that's all."

"Okay," the officer said. "That's good. Now here's what I want the three of you gentlemen to do for me. I want you to start making your way to the door please, nice and slowly, okay? Nice and slowly, don't make a rush of it. Don't give me any reason to be nervous."

"The door's not locked," Jay said. "You can come in if you want."

"I noticed that. But here's the thing – I don't know if you're telling me the truth. And until then, we'll play it my way. Okay? Come to the door gentlemen, all three of you. Walk in single file with your hands up over your heads. Got it?"

"Okay," Jay said. "Whatever you say officer. By the way, one of us is in a wheelchair. Just so you know."

"That's fine."

Iain saw the look in Davie's eyes. That flicker of anger – it was there and gone. Davie didn't appreciate being singled out like that.

Davie was first into the hallway. Jay walked behind him, signalling for Iain to follow. Iain finished his drink first. When he started walking, he realised he was pretty drunk. When was the last time he'd eaten anything?

Oh well, at least he didn't feel the cold anymore.

Why wasn't he relieved? The others were overjoyed at the rescue, but why not Iain? Did he really have so little to go back to in Glasgow that he'd rather stay trapped in the cabin with the fear of death hanging over him?

Didn't matter. It was over now.

He felt empty.

Walking into the hallway, he took a deep breath. Then he turned left.

The policeman was framed in the open doorway, letting a torrent of cold air into the cabin. He wore a standard police cap and a dark fleece, along with a high visibility jacket that had a giant 'POLICE' label stitched at the top.

"Nice and slow chaps," the officer said. "Keep your hands in the air where I can see them."

At the back of the line, Iain's ears pricked up.

That voice. I know that voice.

The three men approached the officer as requested – slow, with hands in the air. The cabin creaked in protest, the wind continued to howl and hiss, as the procession got near the door.

Iain watched as the policeman took his cap off.

He felt an electric chill surge through his body. He might have gasped quietly, then stopped at the back of the line. Thank God he was at the back because at that moment, Iain couldn't conceal the look of shock on his face.

He knew this man.

At last, Iain understood everything. He understood what this was. He understood why he'd been kidnapped and what he was doing in a cabin in the middle of nowhere with Jay Green and Davie Muir. Most importantly, he knew something else.

He knew who the killer was.

12

DAVIE

"Everyone's alright then?" the policeman asked. "Nobody's hurt?"

The officer was tall, about mid-to-late forties, pale skinned with short black hair and a distinctive mutton chop beard that looked like it belonged back in the Victorian age, back when British 'Bobbies' were still chasing Jack the Ripper and riding bicycles. His Scottish accent pitched upwards slightly on the stressed words. East coast? Edinburgh? It was definitely central belt, maybe somewhere in between the nation's two largest cities.

"We're fine," Davie said. "Like Jay said, we're a bit shaken up after everything. But that's about it."

"How did you find us?" Jay asked.

As he spoke, Jay glanced over the officer's shoulder, standing on his tiptoes to get a better view of what was going on outside. Davie couldn't see much from the chair. It was quiet out there, apart from the wind, and he wondered how many of the surviving kidnappers had fled across the hills in these worsening conditions. If the police didn't get them, the weather would. But Davie wanted at least one survivor to pull through this ordeal. He wanted one of these people to take off their masks and to confirm his worst fears about the kidnapping, about the motivation behind the kidnapping.

The thought of never being certain, it would haunt him. But then again, maybe it was best not to know.

"Aye," Davie said, squinting his eyes. "How *did* you find us?"

The officer nodded, acknowledging the question. He briefly studied the rundown conditions of the cabin before answering. The cloudy window with excessive condensation to his left. Three doors running alongside the narrow hallway. The wood rot and mould on the walls and ceiling. Not much to get excited about.

"The station was alerted to the sound of gunshots earlier this morning," he said. "Anonymous caller, someone local. Said they were out walking their dog by the road when they heard a disturbance coming from the old McKenzie cabin."

"The McKenzie cabin?" Davie said.

The officer nodded. "Aye. Archie McKenzie. He hasn't been up here for years though. This old place, it's mostly been forgotten about or so we thought. Seems like somebody still has a use for it."

"I'd like to buy that dogwalker a drink," Jay said, laughing nervously. "I'll get his dog a box of treats too. A year's supply."

Davie pointed over the policeman's shoulder. "The kidnappers. Are they...?"

"Well," the officer said, "it was a bit chaotic sir. Some of them fought right off the bat while others, most of them in fact, ran for their lives. Along the road, up the slopes as if heading for higher ground. Good luck to them in these conditions, they'll need it. There's a lot of rugged country out here and with the snow expected to get worse, they'll freeze to death by nightfall."

Jay's voice was quiet. "Did you see their masks?"

The officer nodded. "I did, aye. What was all that about?"

"Don't know," Davie said. "A bit elaborate if all they wanted to do was hide their faces."

The officer laughed. "I think they wanted to do more than hide their faces. I think they wanted to scare the crap out of you boys."

"Aye," Jay said. "Well, they did a pretty good job." He pointed towards the barren landscape, the last of the green and brown patches vanishing under the snow. "Any idea who they were?"

"I was hoping you could tell me that," the officer said. "You don't know these people? Didn't see a familiar face? A voice?"

Davie shook his head. "We're in the dark. There's a chance it might...that it might be related to our old school. We thought someone might be holding a grudge against the three of us."

"That's one hell of a grudge."

"It's a long story," Jay said. "A very long story."

The officer brushed a covering of snow off the arms of his fleece jacket. "No ransom demands? Nothing like that?"

"They left us a note," Jay said. "It was on the kitchen table when we woke up."

"A note?"

"You want me to go get it?"

The officer narrowed his eyes. "Okay, but be quick about it sir."

Jay nodded. He hurried down the hallway towards the kitchen. When he returned, he offered the note to the policeman. There was a vapid smile on Jay's handsome face.

"That's it."

The officer's eyebrows formed a puzzled arch as he read the note. He looked up at the three men, then glanced at the piece of paper again.

"Is this for real?"

"They shot at us," Davie said. "They've put us through hell. I'd say it's for real, wouldn't you?"

The officer read the note for a third time, his lips silently tracing the words. "*Killer?* That's a big accusation. Has someone here previously been convicted of...?"

"No," Jay said, cutting in.

"I don't understand."

"Join the club," Davie said.

Jay shivered as a fresh gust of cold air flooded the cabin. "Someone's messing with us. It's got something to do with the grudge. From school."

The officer looked up, his nostrils twitching. "Is that whisky?"

"They left us whisky, water and food," Davie said, guessing that the cabin probably smelled like a distillery to a newcomer. "Those were our refreshments while we tried to make sense of this madness. Under the circumstances, we opted for the whisky."

"I don't blame you."

"Aye."

The officer looked puzzled. "This is a most bizarre situation gentleman. I've never seen anything like this before, even when I worked down in Glasgow and Edinburgh where you get all sorts of weirdos."

Jay smoothed down his shirt collar. Patted down his sleeves. "I need to know who's behind this."

"That'll take time sir."

The officer put his cap back on. "Consider yourselves lucky gentlemen. These people went to the trouble of getting you all here. My guess is they would've seen this thing through to the end."

He made a slicing hand motion across his neck.

"It's very remote out here. Three bodies? They can disappear easily."

"Can we get out of here?" Jay asked, edging closer to the door. "I need to call my fiancée and parents. They must be worried sick."

"You can make a call at the station sir."

"Can we go now?"

"We need to comb the area first," the officer said, backing out through the doorway. He raised his voice to be heard over the wind. "It needs to be secured. After that, I'll come and escort you down to the road. Okay?"

"Sure thing," Jay said. "What's another ten minutes going to hurt?"

The officer touched his cap, saluting the three men. "Drink the rest of that whisky lads, you've earned it."

When he was gone, Jay, Iain and Davie, listened to his footsteps receding in the snow. They closed the door. Outside, they heard the policeman talking to someone else, the words muffled, lost in the wind.

"Drink?" Jay asked.

Davie gave him a brief nod. "Aye. It's freezing out here."

They went back to the living room. Jay and Iain sat down on their respective couches while Davie parked his wheelchair in between them. The relief inside the old cabin was palpable. Now the place felt almost hospitable, the closed curtains no longer something to gawp at in terror and confusion. No one flinched every time the walls or floors creaked.

Davie watched a long-legged black spider scurrying across the ceiling. Making its way back to the web.

"The McKenzie cabin, eh?" he said. "Do we know anyone called McKenzie?"

Jay shrugged. "You mean from school? I can't think of anyone off the top of my head but I'm not ruling it out. Can you believe it? Saved by a dogwalker."

Davie laughed. He watched as Jay picked up the whisky bottle and poured a neat dram into everyone's glass. The bottle clinked off the three glasses. If Davie closed his eyes right now, he could have been in a quaint old pub somewhere in the country. Spending time with good friends.

"Aye, usually it's the dogwalkers who find the dead bodies."

"You're not wrong mate," Jay said, relaxing with his glass in hand. He tipped the glass towards him, dipped his nose in and inhaled. "What if that dogwalker decided it was too cold to go out for a walk today? Or they took another route? Jeez man, these little decisions we make, eh? And the big consequences that follow."

Davie glanced over to the other couch. "You alright Iain? You've gone kind of quiet lately."

Iain's nod was weak. "Fine."

"We're getting out man," Davie said, hitting the arm of his chair as if to emphasise the point. "It's over. Now we can drink as much of this stuff as we want. We've actually got something to celebrate."

Jay sat forward, raising his glass in the air. "How about a toast? To old friends and to the killer, whoever he might be."

"To old friends," Davie said.

They clinked glasses and drank.

Jay sighed, stretching out his long legs and putting his feet on the wobbly table. "Well, it's been fun playing junior detective with you guys. Although I don't think the Scottish police missed out on much the day we decided to pursue other careers, eh?"

He laughed again.

"Although Davie, if it turns out Grant Carson's got anything to do with this, I'll buy you guys a slap-up dinner when we get back to the city. I'll make it a five-star restaurant if the big fucker's out there right now, bleeding to death in the snow."

Jay's expression suddenly sobered up.

"To tell you the truth boys," he said, putting his glass on the table. "I'm kind of hoping we can sweep this mess under the table when we get back. I don't want this to be a big thing. Bad timing, you know? If people start asking questions and find out that I was a complete dick at school – that's not a good look for the new CFO at Global. Aye?"

Iain sniggered into the back of his hand. "Truth hurts, doesn't it?"

"What's that mate?"

"Nothing."

Davie held up a stern finger. "Don't fucking start you two. Now this might sound weird boys, but despite everything that's happened, it's actually good to see you again."

"That does sound weird," Jay said, a tight-lipped smile on his face.

Davie nodded, then offered a second toast. "To survival."

"Survival."

Iain emptied his glass, poured out another. He was looking at Davie, occasionally glancing at the chair. "Do you miss Scotland?"

Davie burst out laughing. It was the first time he'd let go since waking up in the cabin that morning. "Are you kidding? I come back for the first time in years and before I've even crossed the border, I get kidnapped, drugged and dumped in a freezing cold cabin with you two fannies. Oh aye, I miss Scotland alright."

Even Iain laughed.

"What about you mate?" Davie asked, when the room was quiet again.

Iain gave a puzzled shrug. "Eh? What about me?"

"You've told me about your job and that, but there's more to life than work. Aye? What else is happening? Are you good?"

Iain stared at the glass in his hand. He was slowly shaking his head. "I don't do much. I don't see many people."

Davie felt the Arctic breeze seeping back into the cabin. Either that or the mood had altered at the flick of some cosmic switch.

It was Jay who spoke. "Why didn't you get married Iain? That's how I always saw it going for you, believe it or not. Decent job, couple of kids, good lady wife – the whole domestic shebang."

"Maybe he didn't want to get married," Davie said, shivering despite the best efforts of the electric heaters and alcohol. "There's no rule that people have to get married, is there? Some people enjoy the single life."

Jay listened, then arched his eyebrows. "Iain? Do you enjoy the single life?"

Iain's cool stare was levelled at Jay over the rim of his glass.

"You live alone," Jay continued, "and you work in the airport shop. Nothing wrong with that and it's not my place to criticise but, just tell me man. I care about you. Would you say that you're happy?"

Iain froze in an uptight sitting position. At the same time, Davie felt a knot tighten in his stomach.

"Something I always wanted to ask you Jay," Iain said in a calm voice. "And now seems like a pretty good time to do it."

"Of course mate," Jay said. "Ask me anything you want."

"This goes back to the summer of 1995. A couple of months after leaving school. I hadn't heard from you."

Iain looked at Davie. The dead eyes were back. "I hadn't heard from either one of you."

Davie felt a sudden desire to leave the room. But that wasn't an option and he knew it.

"It was a long summer," Iain continued, "and I was bored out my skull. I kept wondering to myself, where were my friends? What was with the radio silence? Still, I figured we were all having some chill time after the exams and that we'd catch up soon."

Jay listened, nodding. He looked like someone conducting a job interview with a candidate he'd already dismissed.

"Then," Iain said, his finger running over the rim of the glass slowly, "one afternoon I bumped into your brother in George Square. Imagine my surprise when he told me that you and Davie were on holiday at your aunt's house in the south of France. Remember that house? Big fancy one, you said, with a swimming pool. You were always talking about it in the last year of school. Saying how the three of us were going down there after the exams. The three amigos. Drinking beer. Smoking weed. Hiring a jeep and crossing the border into Spain. You said we'd have mad adventures, Jay. I'll never forget that – mad adventures. I couldn't wait."

Jay leaned back on the couch. Somehow he was still able to maintain eye contact with Iain. "Uh-huh."

"Remember that?"

"Aye, I suppose."

Iain's hand shook as it gripped the whisky glass. Just enough for Davie to notice. "Why didn't you invite me?"

There was a long pause.

"Listen mate," Jay said, glancing at Davie for support. "I don't remember. Look, it was a long time ago. We were what? Seventeen? Eighteen?"

Iain nodded. "I'd still like an answer."

Jay sat up further, his backside sliding towards the edge of the couch. "Oh aye, I remember now. There was only so much space available in my aunt's house at the time. It was a big house but she always had friends and family staying over, especially in the summertime. That's it. I could only take one person with me on that trip. It just happened to be Davie that time. Nothing personal man."

"One person?"

"Aye. That's right."

"Your brother told me that Fiona went too."

Davie couldn't breathe. Game, set and match to Iain. Fiona McNaughton, tall, red-haired and stunning – she *had* been at the house in Toulouse too. Her dad had been a famous welterweight boxer, a world champion in the seven- ties, which made her a terrifying choice for any prospective suitor. But that didn't stop Jay. He'd gone out with her in their sixth and final year at Strathmore. He'd been obsessed. And yes, Iain's information was correct – Fiona had accompanied them on that trip to France, every step of the way. And it had been an incredible holiday. They'd got drunk. They'd smoked weed. Explored. They'd gone to Spain, all the way down to Barcelona. They'd had mad adventures on some days and on other days they sat around the pool lazing in the back garden with Jay's aunt and the other guests.

Davie recalled there being three empty bedrooms during that trip. But he wasn't about to share that with Iain.

"Fiona was my girlfriend back then," Jay said, laughing nervously. "Wherever I went, she went. I figured it was obvious she was there with me."

Iain's gaze drifted off into the corner of the room. "What happened?"

"What's that mate?"

"Why were you guys so quick to drop me after school? I never did get an explanation."

Davie made a brief hand gesture, signalling to Jay that he'd take over.

"It wasn't like that Iain. Honestly mate, it wasn't planned. School was out, it was the end of one chapter and the beginning of something else. Jay and me, we didn't see each other much after the France trip. Right Jay?"

"Right. We just drifted apart. It happens."

Iain's laugh was a wild, high-pitched cackle that came out of nowhere. He punched himself on the leg, several times. "You guys crack me up, you know that? You're so full of shit."

He finished his drink. Then he slammed the glass down like he was trying to break the table.

"Man, are we really forty-four years old?" he said, still giggling. "How did that happen? How can I be a middle-aged man? I was sixteen five fucking minutes ago. I had friends. What happened to me?"

Davie couldn't look at him. He felt like he was going to throw up.

"I missed you guys," Iain said. "I miss what we were.

What we had back then – aye we were dicks, but it wasn't all bad."

Davie wanted to reach out, put an arm around the guy's shoulder and give him a squeeze. He wanted to apologise. But he was terrified that Iain wouldn't take it well.

"Iain," he asked. "Are you okay?"

"I'm sorry about your accident, Davie. I had no idea man."

"Aye. Well, I didn't exactly broadcast it to the world."

"Davie."

"What?"

"Do you ever wish you could go back?" Iain asked.

"To what? The day of the lorry crash?"

"Back to school."

Davie couldn't shake his head fast enough. "Never. Not in a million years mate."

"I want to go back," Iain said. "Every single day of my life, I wish I could go back to a time when..."

The front door creaked open. The cabin groaned under heavy footsteps as a booming voice called to them from the hallway.

"Gentlemen. All clear outside. Are you ready to go to the station?"

Jay leapt to his feet, hurrying to the living room door like a man fleeing a carbon monoxide trap. "Damn right we're ready." He disappeared through the open doorway, turned left and rushed towards the exit. "I can't wait to call home, tell Rachel that..."

The footsteps stopped. The cabin was silent.

And then...

"No."

Davie, who'd been about to yell at Jay for getting up

while Iain was still talking, felt a sudden jolt of fear. "Jay... what is it?"

He toggled the joystick on the right arm of the chair. The chair turned around and raced to the door. He took a left into the hall, heard Iain following close behind.

Davie's heart almost stopped.

The policeman was standing in the hallway, in front of the door. He was dressed in the same police uniform – the black fleece, the high-viz jacket, black trousers and boots. But on his head, instead of the familiar cap, he wore a leathery head mask with orange hair. A matching beard. Feather-trimmed eyeslits.

He had a rifle. And he was pointing it at the three men.

"NO!" Jay yelled, staggering backwards. He almost tripped over the wheelchair and fell onto Davie's lap. His mouth hung open, the words trailing out in a whimper. "No fucking way! No! No! No!"

The man at the door didn't move. "Did you enjoy the show gentlemen?"

Davie felt all the hope deflating inside him. "You sick fucker."

"You're not real police," Jay said, on the brink of tears. "You're not real police. The fucking shootout – what was that about you twisted fucker? What are you doing to us?"

The masked man took a step closer. The hall floor belched under his feet.

"Did it give you hope? Hope of being rescued – hope that someone had come for you when you needed them most? Hope of not having to confess? It's important to have hope in hopeless situations, don't you think? I know all about that."

"Why?" Davie asked. "Why are you doing this?"

"No reason. We're a little bored."

"Bored?"

"Eager to get on with proceedings bud. Let's put it that way. I wanted to come in and find out where you guys were with this thing. How you're progressing. And we also had a little fun – staging the shootout. It was good exercise. Didn't you chaps think it was strange that you didn't hear any sirens?"

"You bastard," Davie said. "Crushing people's hope like that – did it give you a hard on?"

The policeman pulled his mask off, revealing the black hair, mutton chops and handsome pale features. His cheeks were red and glowing. "How close are we to a confession, chaps? It's not that long till sunset. Remember, the sun goes down early in winter."

Jay stabbed the air with his finger. "You shove your fucking confession up your arse dickhead. I don't care if you've got a gun – you're a sick piece of filth and..."

Davie heard an explosion of noise. Sounded like a clap of thunder inside the cabin.

It was Iain who toppled to the floor, screaming at the top of his voice. He gripped his thigh and with bulging eyes, watched as a stream of blood spilled out of his leg, forming a puddle on the wooden floor.

"What the fuck?" Iain howled.

Davie and Jay looked on in stunned silence.

Mutton Chops backed down the hall. On his way to the door, he knelt down and picked up a brown paper package off the floor. He threw it onto Davie's lap.

"Medical supplies. Bandage up the leg. Stop the bleeding."

"Why are you doing this?" Davie said. The wheelchair inched towards the shooter. At that moment, Davie didn't care about anything – the only thing that mattered was finding out what this guy wanted. "Who are you? Who *are* you?"

But Mutton Chops was already outside, closing the door over.

"You have until sunset."

He slammed the door shut. Davie heard the man singing as he walked away from the cabin. Singing loud enough that everyone in the hallway, even over the sound of Iain's screams, could hear him.

It was the same song they'd woken up to earlier that day.

The Verve. 'The Drugs Don't Work.'

13

_____

JAY

Jay helped a bleeding Iain limp back into the living room. He staggered through the doorway, feeling the strain as Iain leaned all his weight against him. Christ, the man was heavy. Blood spilled from his leg. Iain groaned, a pitiful low-pitched drone that barely sounded human. Hurrying inside, Jay guided him over to the couch, sighing with relief as Iain collapsed and transferred his weight onto the spongy cushions.

Davie chased after them both, gripping the brown package.

"Stay awake mate," Jay said. He gave Iain a gentle slap on the cheek. "You're alright. You're going to be fine, I promise. Does it hurt much?"

Iain winced as he lay flat on his back. He had a hand pressed tight against the wound, which it seemed was somewhere on the outside of his left thigh. Blood seeped through his fingers. "It stings like a bitch."

Jay nodded. "Well, we're going to have to take a look." He

unbuckled Iain's belt, popped the button and started pulling Iain's trousers down to the knees. Iain screamed in pain, but didn't try and stop it happening.

Already, Jay's hands were covered in blood. "Davie?"

Davie tore open several layers of brown paper, crudely taped together like a hastily wrapped birthday present.

"I'm on it man."

"What's in there?" Jay asked.

Davie peered inside the package. "Towels, bandages, medication. Here, put this over the wound." He handed Jay one of the towels.

Jay grabbed the towel, unfolded it and placed it over the wound, applying pressure. He didn't know much about first aid but he knew, like most people, that you applied pressure to a bleeder.

"It's alright Iain,' he said. The words felt limp. Cold comfort, but it was the best he could do in the absence of anything more meaningful. Jay had never liked the sight of blood. But right now, there was too much adrenaline flowing to get squeamish. He was performing the right actions. He was doing okay.

"Fuck," Iain said, as Jay handed him the whisky bottle. Iain took a slug, most of which ended up trickling down his chin. "My fucking leg. He shot my leg."

"I know," Jay said. "I know."

It was up to Davie to examine the wound. He got up close in a way that would've made Jay queasy. "The good news," Davie said, probing the splotchy red mess on Iain's leg, "is that the bullet only grazed your leg. That was probably deliberate. Another warning shot."

"Those warning shots are getting more severe each time," Jay said. "You're sure there's not a bullet in his leg?"

"I'm not a doctor. But I don't think so."

Jay felt a massive weight fall off his shoulders. A flesh wound – he could handle that. He'd envisioned them having to pull bullet fragments out of Iain's leg. That wouldn't have been pretty. Flesh wound, okay. That wasn't life or death.

"Bit of bleeding," Davie said in a soothing voice. Jay wondered if that was the voice that Davie used to comfort his kids when they were scared. Would *he* ever get to talk to his child like that? Only if he got out of this nightmare.

Davie was pretty good at the reassuring thing.

"We'll take care of it mate. Okay? You're going to be left with a wee scar on the thigh but you know what they say, eh? Women love scars. You'll be fighting them off with a stick when we get out of here."

That made Iain smile. It only lasted a second before his head dropped back onto the cushion and the grimace returned.

"Good man," Davie said. "Just keep that towel pressed on him Jay."

"Got it."

Jay continued to apply the pressure and they went through another towel before they were satisfied that the bleeding had finally stopped. A flesh wound yes, but a bloody one. Afterwards, they cleaned the wound using a bar of soap from the first aid package and a water bottle from their supply in the kitchen. There was a roll of bandage too and while Jay supported the wounded leg, Davie applied the dressing firmly, but not too tight. He told Jay he was drawing upon the memory of several first aid courses he'd taken years ago. Jay was quietly relieved he didn't have to do it. And while the bandage wasn't expertly applied, it was better than leaving the wound site unprotected.

"Oh God."

Davie reversed the chair back from the couch. Using the

spare bandages, he wiped the blood off his hands. "That was brutal."

"All things considered," Jay said, wiping his brow dry, "we did okay."

Davie assessed the bandage. "Aye, we did."

Jay could still hear the loud whip-crack of the rifle in his head. That could have been him on the couch, bleeding all over the upholstery. Dying, maybe. A victim. He'd been so close to Iain when Mutton Chops squeezed the trigger. Maybe it would be Jay next time. Screw this – he was just a regular guy working a good job down in Glasgow, about to get married, about to start a family. He wanted normal things. Watching Netflix with Rachel. Sunday afternoons visiting his mum and dad for lunch. Restaurants. Shopping trips. Selfies. Walks in the park.

He had to get out of the cabin.

No matter what.

Jay was so deep in thought that he didn't realise he was cleaning his hands on the bloody towels.

"Fuck!" he yelled, throwing it across the room. The towel hit the wall and slid to the floor. Directly above, the black spider was a scrunched-up dot in the cobweb, waiting for flies. Jay envied the simplicity of its existence.

He held his blood-soaked hands up in the air. There was a look of shock on his face, as if he was holding up the bodies of two dead babies. "This has to stop. This HAS to stop. And the only way it's going to stop is if we give these sadistic fuckers what they want. If we don't go along with it, we're going to die."

He lashed out, kicking the flat of his shoe against the wall.

The spider trembled in its web.

"Who are they? Eh? WHO ARE YOU?"

"Jay."

Davie looked tense. He opened his mouth as if to speak, then lowered his head again.

"What is it?" Jay asked. "Is there something you want to tell me or what?"

A pause.

"Nothing. Forget about it"

"Does anyone know how long we've got left?" Jay asked, tapping his wrist where his watch was supposed to be. "Till sunset? It's so fucking cloudy out there, how are we supposed to know?"

"A few hours tops," Davie said. "Maybe less."

Jay pointed to the scant leftovers in the Johnnie Walker bottle. "We drank the entire day away. Lost track of time and achieved a big fat pile of nothing."

It was close now. He was dizzy with the fear of dying. Of being murdered and buried in a shallow grave in a place he didn't know the name of. No, no, no. He was getting out of here tonight and going back to Rachel and the bump at all costs. What sort of state would she be in now? She was pregnant and how did Jay know the masks were telling the truth about putting her back in the house last night? Believe them? Kidnappers? Potential murderers? Add torturers to the list too considering their idea of fun was staging a fake police shootout and spreading false hope.

Jay stared at the bandage on Iain's bloody, naked leg.

Life had never felt so fragile. All pretence of being in control, something that was important to Jay, was gone. It was gone just like that, swept out from under his feet like a rug. Every outcome he faced in his daily life – Jay could see how that outcome was related to a previous choice that he'd made. Control the choices, expect the consequences. That little mantra had worked out pretty well for Jay.

Today, he was blind. He didn't understand why he was here.

"Okay," he said, turning to the others. "We're never going to figure out who's behind this. You know what we're doing here? We're playing guessing games – we're playing guessing games like a bunch of kids. It was them, no it was *them*. No but *they* hated us so much more so it has to be them. Listen guys, our lives are on the line. The only way we're getting out of here is to follow the instructions. We have to give them what they want. And what they want is a confession from the killer."

Jay grabbed the whisky bottle off the floor. He lined the three glasses up on the coffee table, securing the table with one hand while he poured the whisky out with the other. He handed out a glass each, a solemn expression on his tanned face.

"It's truth time," he said.

Jay brought the glass to his lips and knocked back the whisky in one. He felt his stomach burn as the liquid flooded his pipes.

"What are you saying Jay?" Davie asked.

Jay's shirt clung to his skin, sticky with blood and sweat. "Those people are going to kill us. We all see that, right? They didn't do this for nothing. They didn't lock us up and put us through this nightmare for nothing. And now we know for sure, they're not worried about spilling blood."

He tried to get his breathing under control. But right now, his mind was a runaway train lighting sparks on the rail tracks.

"Someone in here's a liar," Jay said. "Someone in here's a killer. I'm willing to bet that somebody in this room did something terrible and so far, you've been hiding it pretty well from the rest of us. This is something that keeps you awake at night. Something that you know you'll never be able to shake off even if you live to be a hundred. Those people out there, the masks, they only want one of us. Why should two innocent men pay for the crime of the third?"

He looked at Davie. At Iain, still flat on his back on the couch, dressed in nothing but boxer shorts and blood below the waist.

Iain rolled his head to the side. His skin was grey and dirty. "Sounds like you're ready to throw someone to the dogs."

"No," Jay said, "I just want to see my kid being born. Is that so wrong? That's why the time for polite conversation is over. Let's not pretend we're still best buddies and that it's 1991, okay? Somebody here has a confession to make."

Jay stared at the bloodstained couch, now just as red as it was cream. For a moment, he was lost in the clash of colours.

"Iain," he said. "Is there anything you want to say?"

Iain barked out a ferocious laugh in response.

Jay shook his head. He pointed to the bandage on Iain's leg where a red Rorschach inkblot stain had formed on the centre of the dressing. "He shot you, Iain. *You*. He could just as easily have shot me or Davie. I was the one mouthing off, so why did he choose you? What does he know about you? Listen, things haven't been going well, have they? You're lonely and lonely people slide into bad habits. They do bad things. Do you take any drugs?"

"Don't talk to me about drugs," Iain snapped. He pushed himself up to a sitting position. Iain's face was so red it looked like his blood vessels were about to explode.

"Take it easy," Davie said.

Jay wasn't sure who Davie was talking to.

But Iain wasn't listening to anyone. He was staring at Jay,

eyes blazing. "You want to talk to me about drugs? Okay. Let's start by reminding ourselves who in this room became a small-time drug dealer after we left school. Was it me? Was it Davie? No, it was...can you guess Jay? Can you guess who it was?"

Jay sighed. "Believe it or not, I care about you, Iain."

"Fuck off," Iain said.

"Talk to me man," Jay said in a calm voice. Although he opened his arms to Iain, he kept his distance. "We were brothers once. All three of us, deep down, we're still brothers. Let me help you man – I can help you get the darkness out and it'll feel so much better when you do. It's choking you up, isn't it? Living alone. No girlfriend. Shitty job. What kind of stuff are you into mate? What do you do for fun?"

Iain spoke through gritted teeth. "I didn't kill anyone."

Jay felt the anger bubbling up inside. It was like hot lava in his veins. He rushed over, grabbed Iain by the collar of his shirt. His hands, still covered in Iain's blood, left smear marks on one of the few areas of Iain's clothing that hadn't turned red.

"Confess."

Iain grinned. "No."

"Confess you fucking little rat. I've got a life to go back to. I've got people who need me. What did you do? Who did you kill? Give me a name Iain, just give me a name."

Iain sprang up to his feet, pushing off his good leg. Jay didn't see it coming. He was pushed backwards, caught by surprise. Iain was off balance when he swung a vicious left hook at Jay's chin. The blow was awkward but landed flush on Jay's cheek. Jay yelped, not in pain but in shock. He staggered backwards across the room, hand pressed to his face.

Hot pain soared to the surface.

"You hit me? You..."

Iain limped manically after Jay with a bloodthirsty glint in his eyes. He closed the gap, pounced and both men fell backwards onto the floor with a sickening crash, their heads missing the edge of the coffee table by inches. Jay felt his back slam against the wooden floor and for a split second, he was in dark place. Then he was awake, covered in blood and sweat and trapped under the weight of Iain.

"Get off me ya fucking psycho!"

Iain had him pinned to the floor.

Jay could hear Davie's voice, a distant protest in the background. "STOP! Iain. Let him go! Will you two just fucking stop it?"

But Iain was too far gone. The guy had been waiting years for this and Jay was certain that if he got the chance, Iain would gladly kill him. Iain hated Jay. Hated everything that Jay had and he didn't. Now he was on top, spitting out a series of savage monosyllabic grunts. His rough hands were wrapped around Jay's neck. He was squeezing down tighter.

There was an insane grin on his face.

Davie was still yelling. Thumping his fist off the padded arm of his wheelchair. "Stop!"

Iain's python-like grip tightened around Jay's neck. Jay made a gagging noise and started hammering on the bloody red bandage on Iain's leg. *Whack-whack-whack!* He clawed at the wound. Carved it up, imagining his fingernails as sharp daggers. Then more punching. Clawing again. His counter-attack was solely aimed at the gunshot wound on Iain's thigh.

"AGHHH!"

Iain finally screamed in pain, unable to take it anymore. He straightened up just as Davie arrived on the scene. Davie, leaning forward, grabbed Iain's fleece top and tried to yank him backwards.

"Get the fuck off him," Davie yelled. "Have you lost your mind?"

Iain shoved Davie backwards. Then he laboured to his feet, leaning heavily on his good leg while pressing a hand against the reddening bandage strapped to his thigh.

"Bastards!" he cried out. "Why did you throw me away like a used toy? What did I do to deserve that? Friends for life, that's what we said. Remember?"

He fell onto the blood-soaked couch. Sitting up, hands over his face, sobbing uncontrollably.

"What the fuck did I do?"

Jay was back on his feet, tentatively touching at his bruised neck. His voice was raspy. Each syllable uttered was like swallowing a pebble.

He couldn't stop now.

"Who did you kill Iain?"

Iain spat in Jay's direction. His face was a twisted mask of pure loathing. "I fucking hate you. I hate you."

Jay took a step forward, convinced that Iain was on the brink of confessing. Of spilling his guts once and for all. At the same time, he kept one arm extended in between them, in case Iain pounced again.

"Confess."

"No."

"Do it Iain. You'll feel so much..."

"Stop."

It was Davie.

Jay shook his head. "We need to make him talk. Look at him, he's ready to go. We're almost out of here."

"This has gone far enough," Davie said. "Stop it. No more. I need to tell you guys something...something I should have told you hours ago."

"What?" Jay croaked back. With his raspy voice, he

sounded like something out of *Star Wars*. "What are you talking about?"

Davie's mouth twitched at the side. He shook his head, mumbled under his breath. "I wanted to tell you."

Both Jay and Iain turned towards Davie. He looked back at them both, a pained smile on his face.

"It's me."

Jay's throat burned as he nervously swallowed. "Eh? What are you...?"

Iain sat forward. Wiped his eyes dry. "Davie, what are you saying?"

In that moment, Davie's face was as white as the snow on the ground. His expression as grim as it had ever been, which was saying something when it came to Davie. When he finally spoke, his voice was little more than a whisper.

"I'm the killer."

14

DAVIE

It was too late to go back. Davie had opened the door and now he'd have to walk the others through it.

They stared at him. Gawped, as if he'd grown a third eye.

"Something happened on the day of the lorry crash. Something besides the crash itself, all those people hurt or dead, and me getting crippled. It's something I don't want to think about, let alone talk about."

Davie's knuckles whitened as he made a pair of tight fists. He took a deep breath, not sure if he had it in him to do this.

"Argyle Street. Five years ago, almost to the day. I suppose it was about two o'clock on the Saturday afternoon, one of those sunny wintery days where all the buildings, the intricacies of the architecture, were lit up with sunlight. The city was buzzing, crowded with Christmas shoppers getting in there early."

He paused.

"Can I get a drink?"

Jay nodded. He grabbed the bottle of Johnnie Walker and, although there wasn't much left, poured a small measure into Davie's glass. Davie mumbled his gratitude, took a drink and felt the whisky burn his oesophagus. He longed for more but he knew an entire bottle wouldn't be enough.

"That first scream – I didn't think much of it. You know what it's like when it's busy in town, especially at the weekend, especially when the sun's out. People go crazy. I thought it was just someone having a laugh with their mate, you know? Then the second and third scream..."

The whisky couldn't stop his voice trembling.

"The lorry driver had blacked out at the wheel after a set of traffic lights. Everything after that was bad luck – the worst luck. The lorry squeezed in between a set of lights and bollards where there was just enough room to mount the pavement. If it had tried to get up anywhere else the bollards would have stopped it. They say it travelled for about twenty seconds at twenty-five-miles per hour. Doesn't sound much, does it? The screaming was awful. The lorry hit street poles, scraped off the wall, but somehow it kept going. It was the people who never saw it coming – they were the ones who..."

Davie listened to the wind outside. His mind drifted back to that terrible day.

"Everyone panicked. And when you panic, you don't think. You react. Those of us in close proximity to the lorry when it first mounted the kerb, if we'd all jumped over the metal fence at the edge of the pavement and landed on the road, it couldn't have touched us. We didn't. Most people ran straight ahead. Shouting and pushing, trying to make room. It was like the lorry was the predator and everyone on the pavement was the prey."

"Davie," Jay said, his tone mildly impatient. "What happened? What is it you're trying to tell us?"

Davie lowered his head.

"There was a woman in front of me. We were both running, she was slowing me down and I kept clipping her heels. I thought she was going to knock me off my feet. All I wanted to do was to make room. Room to get past her. So, I shoved her. I didn't mean to knock her off her feet. I swear to God, I didn't mean it."

Jay and Iain exchanged puzzled glances.

"What's that got to do with this?" Jay asked.

"She had a partner. He was running just ahead of us, looking back, making sure that the woman was still there. He must have seen me shoving her. And when she went down, I heard him yell, curse, scream – all of it. I'll never forget the look on his face. The way he looked at me. This was all happening in a matter of seconds."

"She died?" Jay asked.

Davie nodded. "I saw her go under the front wheels. Her partner, he saw it too."

Jay poured some more whisky into Davie's glass. Davie's hand was shaking so much he could barely pick it up.

"What about the guy?" Jay said. "The woman's partner. Did he...?"

"Aye, he survived. I don't know how he did it but he must have jumped the fence and got onto the road. Maybe he's got the reflexes of a cat, who knows? I stayed on the pavement and the lorry kept coming. I was one of the last people hit before it finally came to a stop. Spinal cord injuries. The rest is history, but I lived. The coward lives. Meanwhile, an innocent woman dies."

Davie hung his head. He felt like he was waiting for the death sentence to be read out.

"You're not a coward," Jay said. His voice was strangely matter-of-fact considering what Davie had just told him.

"I am."

"No, you're not. In life-or-death situations like that Davie, few people ever live up to their values. Reality has that effect sometimes. Remember that big ferry disaster in the nineties? The boat that sank, what was it called? *Estonia*? It was all over the news at the time and I read shocking things about what people did that day to save their own skin. People trampling over kids and the elderly. It's not evil, it's not cowardice either. It's a built-in primitive survival instinct that we have no control over. We're animals and all animals care about self-preservation."

"What's it got to do with us?" Iain asked, still pressing down on his bandage. "With this? Why we're here."

"I saw him at the second memorial," Davie said, "one year after the crash. I missed the first one because I was still in hospital. But there he was and I could see that he recognised me. Just seeing him, it brought it all back. Nothing happened but about a week later, I saw him near my house. Just standing around. Loitering, hands in his pocket. The weird thing is, he never came up to me. Never said a word. There was no actual confrontation, you know? I saw him on the street the next day and the day after that."

"He was stalking you?" Jay asked.

"Aye. And I became paranoid, convinced he was planning to go after Elena and the kids. I got a mate in the police to do a bit of digging. We found out his name – Tam Mills, a motorbike mechanic, originally from Troon. Turned out he's a hunting nut too. Knew all about guns and with a pack of mates, he took regular trips to the Highlands to shoot rabbits, deer and God knows what else."

Davie leaned back in the wheelchair.

"On my mate's recommendation," he said, "we moved to the Southside. Mills found me in less than a week. The police tried to scare him off but it never lasted. Looking back, I think he was trying to drive me insane. Keep me on edge twenty-four hours a day."

"Is that why you moved to London?" Jay asked. "To get away from him?"

"Aye. That was the main reason."

Jay pushed a clump of sweat-soaked hair off his forehead. "Fucking hell, Davie. Why didn't you say anything before? A hunting nut with a grudge? A guy who goes on regular killing sprees with his mates? And he knows the Highlands?"

Davie didn't answer.

"If it *is* Tam Mills out there," Jay said, jerking his thumb towards the window. "Then why am I here? Why's Iain here?"

"The school connection," Davie said. "It's a false trail for anyone who comes looking for us. It's the perfect cover."

"Mutton Chops," Jay said. "The fake policeman who shot Iain's leg. Did you...?"

"No. I've never seen him before."

Davie's whisky-soaked haze was wearing off. The confession to Jay and Iain felt good but he knew that he had to go outside and do it all over again, to give Tam Mills what he wanted. Davie would admit his wrongdoing that day when he'd pushed the poor woman to her death. He'd admit that he was a killer.

But would it be enough?

There'd be punishment afterwards. Most likely, it would be death and then what for Iain and Jay? Would Mills forget about Elena and the children? Davie would try and get the man's word before it was over. His death would be the end of it. His family had done nothing wrong and they *had* to be left alone. Iain and Jay didn't deserve to die either. Maybe there was still hope for them.

He moved towards the door. "I'm going outside."

Jay tilted his head. "You're doing what?"

"Mills wants a confession. Then he's going to shoot me for what I did. Before he does that, I'll talk him into letting you go."

Davie pushed the joystick, taking the chair into the hallway and towards the front door. The cold crept under his skin. It was invasive, aggressive and it wouldn't have surprised Davie one bit to discover that the old Mackenzie shack was haunted. This was the sort of cold that took your senses away.

Faint, muffled cries chased after him. But Davie wondered, how sincere were Jay and Iain in calling him back? The three men in the cabin, once friends, were now total strangers. And the other two had to be happy that he was going outside to make the confession because that meant their ordeal would soon be over. Unless of course, they were all dead men. But they'd only seen Mutton Chops' face so far. There was hope.

Jay was in the hallway now. "Davie. Wait!"

Davie slowed the chair to a stop. But he didn't turn around.

"I think about her all the time. About what I did, what I took from her. I think about Michelle Carson too. Actually, I googled her name a while back. I found one thing online about her. *One thing* on a disused forum for former Strathmore Academy students who want to keep in touch after school. Just a couple of lines that some idiot wrote years ago. *Remember Michelle Carson? She was the crazy bitch who jumped off a bridge.* And that's it. Two lines, written by a fucking moron."

"Davie," Jay said. "We didn't put those scratches on her arm. You can't blame yourself for everything that happened."

Davie looked over his shoulder. Jay was standing beside the living room door.

"You want to see your kid being born. Don't you?"

"I do."

"See you Jay."

Davie drove the chair to the door and pulled it open. He backed up, made room and steered through the open doorway. The cold was bitter. But he kept going, riding over the paved area that was covered in snow. He had to plough forward although he risked getting stuck. By the morning, he figured, this place would be buried under an avalanche. The snow was thicker and more impenetrable further away from the door, bringing Davie's advance to a halt.

He cupped his hands over his mouth.

"I'm here!"

His eyes combed the rugged landscape. He knew that somebody was out there, watching, listening, waiting for the moment of truth. They'd show up soon, one of them, most likely all of them in their fancy-dress costumes. As Davie waited, he gazed at the lumpy white hills, the loch, and the grey sky blanketed with menacing clouds. The wind howled, blowing his hair back off his face.

It was as good a place to die as anywhere.

He shivered in the seat. Thought about his wife and children all the way down in London and how he hoped they'd understand, that's if they ever found out the truth. But if Mills left them alone, then it was worth it.

His thoughts were interrupted by footsteps.

Davie saw them emerge from the wintery gloom, walking towards the cabin at an excruciatingly slow pace. They wore their masks, along with the long winter coats that trailed to their boots. The leader, along with several others, carried a rifle. The weapons were lowered at their sides. For now.

"Are you ready to confess?" the leader yelled. Davie was certain that it was Mutton Chops' deep voice under the mask.

Davie nodded. "It's me. I'm the killer."

"Go on," the leader said, his muffled-sounding voice battling to be heard in the wind. "What do you confess to?"

Davie sat there in the freezing cold, telling the masks the same story he'd told Jay and Iain inside the cabin. But he didn't stop after the Argyle Street tragedy. He told them about the things he'd done in school. He told them about Michelle Carson and how she jumped off the Erskine Bridge with scratches all over her arms and legs. About all the other people whose lives he'd ruined as the brains behind the Lads. This was his confession and Davie couldn't stop talking after holding back all those years. He let it go, hoping that it meant something. For Elena, the kids. For Jay and Iain.

When he was done cataloguing his sins, Davie fell back in his seat exhausted. His thoughts turned back to his family and the soft, comforting sensation of snowflakes landing on his face and hair. It felt good. Felt clean. He thought about his dad who'd been dead for thirty years. It wouldn't be so bad, he thought. To die now, after unburdening himself.

The masks were silent. The leader stared at Davie through feathery eyeslits.

"What are you waiting for?" Davie asked. "You got what

you wanted, didn't you? Now keep your word – let the others go. And leave my people alone."

The leader raised his rifle to a firing position. The barrel was pointing at Davie as he walked forward.

"Mills?" Davie said, bracing himself for the end. He was desperate to know. "Tam Mills? Are you here?"

When the man peeled the mask off his face, it was Mutton Chops looking at Davie. There was a strange, look of knowing on the kidnapper's face. A serene expression that Davie couldn't understand.

"You confess?"

"I confess," Davie said again.

Mutton Chops backed away with slow, deliberate steps. He shook his head, lowering the rifle to his side.

"I confess," Davie yelled. "I confess!"

"But it's the wrong confession," Mutton Chops called out. "This is not the confession we're looking for."

Davie's jaw dropped. It felt like he'd punched in the face.

Mutton Chops pointed a gloved finger over Davie's shoulder. "Go back inside the cabin," he said. "Go back, tell your friends what happened. Tell them, time is running out. I want that confession Davie, I want it."

PART III

THE KILLER

15

JAY

Looking at Davie in the aftermath of his failed confession, Jay might as well have been looking at a statue of the man.

The last thing Davie told the others before he'd clammed up was that Mutton Chops had rejected his confession. That was it, but it was enough. He *wasn't* the killer after all. Now the wheelchair was parked in front of one of the two electric heaters, Davie thawing out in silence. He sat with his shoulders slumped, head flopped forward like a deflated doll.

Jay's blood froze in his veins as he processed the news. After almost a full day in the cabin, speculating and drinking whisky on empty stomachs, one of the three Lads had been eliminated from the race.

Now, Jay and Iain stared at one another from opposite ends of the room. Jay was once again, pacing slowly from side to side. Iain, no doubt exhausted after all the blood he'd lost, was conserving his energy on the couch. He was just sitting there, a blood-soaked hand placed over his bandage.

The man looked strangely at peace. Was it the wound? Was he delirious with blood loss? Jay, on the other hand, couldn't keep still. His heart was slamming off his rib cage. He felt like he was on the brink of blacking out.

"It's you or me mate," Jay said, his voice cracking with tension. "That's what it's come down to. And I know it's not me they're waiting for out there. In fact, as God as my witness, I'll swear on my unborn kid's life that I haven't killed anyone."

"Do you believe in God?" Iain asked.

Jay pointed a finger at Iain. "What are you willing to swear on? Eh? C'mon mate, we're running out of time."

Iain laughed. Another of those out of the blue, hyena-like cackles.

"You can't help yourself, can you? Can't stop being a slimy know-it-all prick for five minutes, aye?"

"What are you going on about?"

"You're a cunt, Jay. That's what I'm going on about. You're a Judas dressed up as a fucking Ken doll!"

"I'm just telling it like it is," Jay said. "I'm also trying to keep my emotions in check, which maybe you should do too."

He couldn't back down to this psycho. Couldn't show any weakness. The threat of violence was in the room and Jay could taste it. He knew that Iain, despite his wounded leg, was thinking about it too.

"Iain – listen to me. I'm going to be a dad."

"You've said that like a hundred times already."

"Yes I have. Do you understand what that means? I've got people who depend on me. I've got a fiancée. I've got a baby coming into the world and he needs his dad. Iain, just do the right thing. Please. Will you do the right thing?"

Iain snatched the Johnnie Walker bottle off the table.

His face screwed up in disappointment when he saw it was empty. He tipped it back anyway, consuming the last few precious drops and then he tossed the bottle onto the couch.

His face was frozen in a menacing snarl.

"Never killed anyone, have you Jay? Bullshit. What about me? You killed me after we left school, you killed me when you and Davie boy and your ginger bitch went off to France without me."

Jay's hands cut the air in a slicing motion.

"Shut up," he yelled. He could feel his headache coming back. "Stop fucking whining about the past, will you? You're the killer and I've known it from the start. Everyone here knows it. Now look – you've had too much whisky and you're in shock after getting shot. Think clearly Iain, think clearly. What did you do?"

Iain got up, staggered his way around the coffee table. He was still dressed only in boxer shorts from the waist down and he winced every time his wounded leg hit the floor.

"My mind's clear."

"Listen to yourself," Jay said. "You're slurring your words. Can you hear how much you're slurring your words?"

Jay glanced at Davie, searching for help. Perhaps Davie, as he'd done so many times before, would say the right thing to ease the tension. But Davie was a ghost. His eyes were open, staring into empty space as he sat thawing beside the heater. He looked like a broken version of himself.

"Iain," Jay said. "I'm sorry if I hurt you back then. But Jesus man, I didn't realise you had such an axe to grind about stuff that happened over twenty years ago. I'm sorry your life turned out to be so shit but it's not my fault. And it's not Davie's fault either. You can't blame your old school pals for every single thing that went wrong in your life after the final exam ended. *Oh, my life sucks because the Lads aren't the Lads anymore.* What? Were we supposed to keep the gang together through college, through work and into retirement?"

"Yes!" Iain yelled. "Why not?"

"Really? Was that your dream? The three of us glued together in a care home in our eighties? Flushing all the other OAP's heads down the toilet for a giggle?"

Hard words, but Iain needed to hear this. Jay should have said it twenty-five years ago, this and a whole lot more. He should have told Iain to his face that he didn't want to know him anymore. That would have been the end of it. And never in a million fucking years would he have invited Iain to France.

"You were useful back then, okay? You looked tough and that counts for something in the school playground. Back when a teenage boy's life is a twenty-four hours a day dick-measuring contest. But after that? I didn't need you. I didn't need a dead-eyed heavy trailing after me like a fucking shadow. Accept it, Iain. Accept that people move on with their lives. You couldn't evolve because the world expanded beyond the school fence. Well, I'm very sorry but I've got a fiancée, a baby on the way and..."

"I met a girl," Iain snapped. He was unsteady on his feet, swaying from side to side. "She's called Alison."

"Okay," Jay said, nodding his head. "That's good. So you *do* want to get out of this?"

Iain grunted in the affirmative.

"Remember the note?" Jay asked, trying to take all the anger out his voice. "The note said if the killer confesses then we all go home."

"You don't really believe that, do you?"

"Yes I do," Jay said. "We give Mutton Chops what he wants and I go home to my people, Davie goes back to London and you get to go back to Alison, wherever she is. C'mon Iain, are you ready to man the fuck up?"

Iain was laughing again. Jay felt like someone was twisting a sharp knife around in his guts.

"You remember that time in third year?" Iain said. "Fraser Dowell and his mates, one year older than us, built like tanks the lot of them. Remember? They were waiting for you after school, Jay. Waiting for *you* because you'd called Dowell's sister a fat whore."

Jay shrugged. "Iain, how is this relevant?"

Iain's smile began to wane. "You found out that he was after you and you shat your pants man. You were so scared. Everyone knew that Dowell was going to wait for you at the gate after school. On Maple Drive, remember? Everyone heard about it. Everyone was going there to watch because they wanted to see Jay Green get his head kicked in."

"Iain..."

"Three o'clock came and the bell rang. You were panicking. You told me and Davie you wanted to avoid Maple Drive at all costs. Go that way instead, go this way – anywhere to avoid the fight."

"Iain..."

Iain thumped his chest. "We were the ones that stepped up that day. Me and Davie, we insisted on going down there to face Dowell and his gang head on. We told you we couldn't run away, no matter what. We had to square up to them otherwise everyone in school would know that we shat it. And after that, the Lads would be finished."

"Iain, what the fuck has this got to do with your confession?"

"I had your back that day!" Iain yelled, his eyes bulging

with anger. "I looked out for you and what happened to Dowell? We beat the shit out of his gang and everyone saw it. *I* beat the shit out of Dowell himself and the Lads were stronger and better and had more respect, because of me. *Me*."

Iain's voice dropped to a hoarse whisper.

"I showed you so many times that I was capable of getting shit done. And you dropped me anyway. Well, guess what? I'm ready to get shit done again."

"You're going to confess?" Jay asked.

Iain limped towards the door. He was laughing again. "Wait and see Jay, wait and see. You're going to love this man."

"Iain?" Davie said, snapping out of his trance. "What are you doing?"

But Iain didn't answer. He was hobbling towards the door, pale and weak, but determined to get out there. A second later, the front door groaned open. Then the piercing sound of the wind entering the hallway, bringing a nightmarish cold with it.

"We'd better go after him," Davie said.

Jay nodded. "Aye."

The front door was lying ajar when they got there. Davie and Jay made their way outside, hurrying into the freezing cold and just in time to see the dull outline of Iain walking away from the cabin. He was plodding purposefully through the snow towards the masks who were already waiting.

Distant storm clouds had gathered above the pear-shaped loch. The sun, somewhere behind the darkening canvas overhead, was well on its way down.

"Iain," Jay hissed over the shrieking wind. "What are you doing?"

Iain stopped in front of the crowd of masks. Jay sensed

that there were more of them than there'd been before. Quite a lot more.

The mask at the front removed his disguise and Jay recognised Mutton Chops, the bastard who'd toyed with them earlier. Jay was going to bury this bastard somehow. In court, on the street – it didn't matter. He'd always remember that face. And once he got out of here, he wouldn't rest until he'd caught up with him again.

"Is the killer ready to confess?" Mutton Chops asked.

Iain glanced over his shoulder, eyes lingering on his old friends. "Yes."

"Then confess."

"I'm the killer."

"Repeat please,' Mutton Chops said, raising his voice. "The weather's getting worse. I think some of us might have missed that."

"I'm the killer!" Iain yelled, louder this time.

There was a long silence in which nobody seemed to move. Jay stood outside the cabin, wondering what the hell was going on – had some mischievous god in the heavens pressed the pause button on this terrible scene?

The masks, huddled together in the background, burst into a sudden round of applause. It lasted about a minute and when it was over, the eerie congregation tore off their masks and in unison, tossed them up in the air like they were students at a graduation ceremony.

Jay could see them now. Their faces were so ordinary.

"I knew it," Jay said. "It was Iain. It was always Iain."

Davie nodded. "So what now?"

A tall, red-haired woman emerged from the crowd. To Jay's horror, she walked past Mutton Chops and made her way over to Iain with her arms outstretched. She was beautiful and smiling. Iain rushed over to meet her. He was calling to her. Saying her name over and over again.

Alison.

They fell into each other's arms.

Jay felt like he was going to throw up. "Oh my God. He knows them. Davie, he knows them."

Davie said nothing.

"Iain," Alison said, her face glowing with pride. "You did it."

Iain held her tight as if Alison was the dream that he didn't want to ever wake up from. "I did it."

She stepped back, breaking the embrace. The smile remained on her ashen face as she glanced over at Jay and Davie for a few seconds. Then she turned back to Iain. "Now there's only one thing left to do. Are you ready?"

"Iain," Mutton Chops yelled, loud enough to start an avalanche. "You've confessed. Are you ready to be born again?"

A loud cheer from the crowd encouraged Iain to pump his fist in the air. He was grinning, Jay noticed. Grinning like a lunatic. These people, they *loved* him.

"I'm ready."

Mutton Chops smiled. "Iain, tell everyone gathered here what they want to know. Who did you kill, Iain? Say it loud, who did you kill?"

When Iain turned back to the cabin, there was a look of rapture on his face.

"I killed Jay Green," he said. "And I killed Davie Muir."

16

IAIN
Nine months earlier

Alison was waiting for Iain when he walked into The Old Tavern. She looked every bit as good as he remembered. Her long red hair had been washed; it was still damp, hanging loose over her shoulders. Her milky blue eyes lit up when she saw him and she stood up at the table. Waved him over, the gesture dripping with enthusiasm. Alison was tall, a few inches taller than Iain, and even in the casual jeans and jumper combo that she had on, she still oozed a certain elegance.

Iain loved the cute dimples that appeared when she smiled.

He waved back, let her know that he'd seen her.

He walked over to where Alison was sitting at a small corner table, along with two of her male friends. A pint of lager sat untouched beside the empty chair.

Iain loved The Old Tavern. The pub, with its stone walls and giant fireplace, had a friendly atmosphere that Iain could never find in Glasgow pubs. Not that he went to pubs there much anymore.

Here, everyone knew each other.

"Iain," Alison said, wrapping him up in a warm embrace. She gave the best hugs. Afterwards, she kissed him on the lips and Iain could smell the forest, the earth and the sweet salt on her skin.

It wasn't crowded tonight in the Tavern, just a few people scattered here and there minding their own business. Some playing draughts or chess. Most however, were talking or watching a TV in the corner of the room that was showing a football match. English Premiership. Iain didn't know who was playing – he didn't care much for football anymore. There was a blackboard sign behind the bar with a chalk scribble that promised live ceilidh music later that night. Iain made a mental note to stick around. He'd never been disappointed by the entertainment in the Tavern.

"You remember Jonas," Alison said, gesturing to the massive blond man at the table.

Iain nodded. He did recognise Jonas from a previous visit, but not the other guy sitting with them. Jonas was a big, bulky German with a blond mullet that harked back to the mid-eighties. He was originally from Munich and from what Iain could remember about their brief conversations last time, he'd been a paramedic, as well as a landscape gardener and a waiter, before he'd packed up and travelled west across Europe. A seeker, that's how he described himself nowadays.

The other man with the black crewcut and distinctive mutton chop beard was a stranger to Iain. He was handsome and well-groomed and he had striking eyes, which Iain didn't like. He also didn't like the fact that this man was sitting beside Alison. Fortunately, Iain knew better than to get jealous. Alison wasn't the sort of shallow woman to get hung up on looks. Iain was training himself to be secure in their relationship. There had to be trust if it was going to work. That's what all the websites said anyway.

Iain shook hands with the big German. It was like shaking hands with a grizzly bear.

"And this," Alison said, gesturing to the second man, "is Harris. He's the one I told you about last time. The one I've been desperate for you to meet."

Harris stood up and they shook hands. He was pretty tall, much more suited height-wise to Alison than Iain was. Iain felt another stab of jealousy, but when Harris smiled it was the same genuine smile that was typical of all of Alison's friends. At the least the ones he'd met so far in Gairloch. Since the beginning of his road trips, Iain had fallen in love with the village almost as much as he'd fallen in love with Alison. It was incredible – the awe-inspiring scenery, the sandy beaches and the rocky coastline. It was paradise up here. After only three visits, he'd amassed a small group of friends too. This was where he belonged.

"When did you get in?" Alison asked, as everyone sat down again.

Iain unzipped his jacket. Hung it over the back of the chair. "Last night, around eight."

"Same bed and breakfast?"

"Aye, up at the View. I like it there."

"Mrs Buchanan's nice, eh?"

"Aye. She's always fussing and that, but she takes good care of her guests."

Jonas took a loud slurp of lager. He wiped the froth off his beard and grinned. "So Iain. You're falling in love with this place, ya? Just like I did."

"Aye," Iain said, glancing at Alison. He didn't understand

why Harris got to sit beside her, especially when he'd travelled all this way. Still, it was his fault for showing up late. He took a sip of lager, hoping that the alcohol would ease his constant blushing.

"You look familiar Iain," Harris said, his eyes probing across the table. "Have we met before?"

Harris's accent was different to most of the Gairloch people. More central belt, possibly Glasgow or the surrounding areas.

Iain shook his head. "I don't think so."

Harris nodded, seemingly accepting the answer. He picked up his pint and leaned back in the chair. "Been up to Gairloch a few times now?"

"Aye."

"Cool. Alison said she's explained a wee bit about us. About what we've got going on up here. About our little community."

Harris wasn't talking about the regular Gairloch community. Iain knew that much.

"A bit, aye."

Harris and Alison exchanged subtle glances. Iain saw it and although his left brain told him it was nothing, it still felt like a dagger to the heart. *Why were they sitting together?* Harris, perhaps sensing the inappropriateness of his behaviour, quickly turned his attention back to Iain.

"You see Iain," he said, "it's much more than a community. It's a family. And if what Alison tells me about you is true, then I suspect we're exactly what you've been looking for."

Iain nodded. "Aye, maybe."

"I know we've just met," Harris said, blushing slightly himself now, "but I'm the sort of person who likes to cut to the chase. Don't think of this as a formal interview buddy, okay? We just need to know a few things about you before we go any further. Ask a few questions. Is that alright?"

"Aye, go for it."

Alison was beaming at Iain across the table. "You'll be great. Just be honest."

"How are things at home?" Harris asked.

Iain picked up the glass of lager. It was freezing cold and he brought the rim slowly to his lips. "Ermmm..."

"Would this be easier if it was just the two of us?" Harris asked. Before Iain could answer, Harris nodded. "I get it bud – it feels like an interrogation, right? Nae bother. We've all been there my man. Jonas, Alison – would you mind giving Iain and I a couple of minutes please? This won't take long."

Jonas nodded. "Of course, ya."

The German gorilla pushed his chair back, mumbling something about getting another round of drinks in. Alison stood up too, scooping her handbag off the corner of the chair. She slung the strap across her shoulder. "Guess I'll go powder my nose then."

"Cheers pal," Harris said. "Come back in about five minutes, eh?"

Alison touched Iain on the shoulder as she walked past him. Iain twitched at the surge of electricity in his body.

"So, where were we?" Harris asked, when it was just the two of them. There was a strange analytical intensity to the man's gaze that unsettled Iain.

"Can't remember."

"I'm very direct," Harris said, leaning his head forward. "I get that, but small talk isn't really my thing. And I hope you don't mind me saying but I sense a massive weight on your shoulders, aye? Feels like you've been carrying it around for years."

Iain shrugged.

"Know how I know that? Because I was a lost soul once too, living a very different life to the one I'm living now. You should have seen it bud. I was a dreamer – I've always been a dreamer. I had the brains and the vision to go far, but I got involved with heavy drugs after I left school. It was bad. A downward spiral that lasted a few years. The big 'H', you know? I was injecting and everything. I very nearly died."

His smile waned for a moment.

"I got past it. I lived – somehow. Afterwards though, I couldn't adjust to the life that others wanted to shove down my throat. It made me think about why I'd gotten into heroin in the first place. To escape from this shite society – a society that I felt nothing for. *Nothing.* I didn't like what I was seeing out there, what I was surrounded by. Capitalism. Consumerism – it's eating us alive, crushing our spirits and convincing us at the same time that we're loving it. And my family wanted me to become a part of that?"

Iain wanted Alison back at the table.

"I don't mind talking in front of the others. Can they come back now?"

Harris nodded. "Okay bud. Cool, no worries."

He signalled over to the bar, letting Jonas know that it was safe to come back. A moment later, Jonas returned to the table with four pints of lager on a tray. He put the lagers down, went back to the bar and after exchanging another round of friendly banter with the barmaid, came back with four whiskies.

"You're safe with us," Jonas said, sliding a whisky in front of Iain. "That's Glenfiddich by the way. The good stuff, ya?"

Iain smiled, relieved that he was no longer alone with Harris.

"Cheers."

Jonas gave Iain a playful tap on the shoulder as he sat

down. "My life was a mess until I found these people. On the surface, I should've been happy. I had money in Germany, I had a family, a good job, and none of it satisfied me on a deeper level. I was miserable, drifting down, getting caught up in all kinds of bad shit by the time I arrived in London. That's where Sharon, another member of our community, found me. After that, she brought me up here to paradise. It got better for me – much better. The healing, it's real. Harris is the best teacher I've ever known and being in the Hand, it's the happiest I've ever been."

Iain frowned. "The Hand?"

"Every community needs a name," Harris said. "We chose the Hand of Glory, to give it its full title. Named after a good luck charm from olden times, the preserved hand of a hanged man. Here, take this."

Harris slid something across the table. It was a carved wooden keyring of a closed fist with a candle tucked in between the fingers.

Iain picked it up and smiled. "That's pretty cool."

"The Hand of Glory is said to provide light to its bearer," Harris said. "We are the awakened ones. Meanwhile everyone else who sleeps, sleeps deeper. As I said, the original charms were supposedly taken from the corpse of a hanged man. It's an object, severed from the dead. And that's how I perceive our community, as something unshackled from a corpse."

Alison returned from the bathroom. Once aboding, she caressed Iain's shoulder before taking her place at the table. She took a sip of whisky and glanced at each of the three men.

"We good?"

Harris nodded, then turned back to Iain. "Be honest with us – we're about to become your family after all."

Jonas slid the whisky into Iain's hand. "Have some courage," he said, pointing to the glass. Iain nodded, drank the whisky like it was a shot. His throat burned and he felt fuzzy in the head.

"Here goes," he said, twirling the keyring chain around his fingers.

Alison smiled. "From the heart sweetie. From the heart."

Iain nodded, then cleared his throat. "I've got nothing. I've been living a miserable life for years and I have no one. My family don't want to know me. I'm not a good person though, so maybe this is the outcome I deserve."

Harris's eyes narrowed. "What makes you think you're not a good person?"

"I was a bully in school," Iain said. "I treated people like shit and because of that, I suppose it's karma. There were three of us back then and we were right fucking bastards to the other kids. That's putting it mildly. The way I see it, we never got punished back then so maybe it's just catching up with me twenty-five years later."

"What school did you go to?" Harris asked.

"Strathmore Academy. In the southside of Glasgow."

There was a subtle change in Harris's expression. Up until then, the man's face had been a serene mask but now there was something else creeping in. His smile narrowed at the corners. His eyes dulled. This was a different kind of interest.

"Strathmore?" he said. "I know that school – I know it pretty well in fact."

Iain nodded. "It's a shithole."

"What's your full name bud?" Harris asked, after taking a sip of whisky. His eyes never left Iain. "If you don't mind my asking."

"Iain Lewis."

"Uh-huh. You said something about being a bully at school, aye? That there were three of you? The others – what were their names?"

Iain wondered if this was still part of his initiation. "Davie Muir and Jay Green."

Again, the man's expression changed. This time, a light went back on in his eyes and Iain wasn't sure he liked the way that Harris was grinning across the table. It was the smile of a hungry man who'd just smelled food.

"Jason 'Jay' Green? Tall, dark and handsome, right?"

"You know him?"

"I did once, yep."

Harris glanced at Alison, exchanged a knowing look. "Never mind about that anyway," he said. "Back to you Iain. Tell me, what do you think of our little family so far? Of Alison, Jonas and the others you've met since you started coming up here?'

"I like it."

That was an understatement. But he didn't want to appear too desperate if he hadn't already.

"And you haven't seen the village yet? I mean, *our* village."

"No."

"It's very remote. Even for around these parts."

"I like the sound of that," Iain said. "I'd like to see it. More than anything else, I'd like to become a part of it."

"Another finger for the Hand," Jonas said, patting Iain on the back. "Why not? We could use a good man like you."

Iain looked at Alison. She smiled, her face glowing with an almost maternal pride.

Harris closed his eyes, like he was about to start praying. "Minimal technology. It's quiet and we're a real community with bonds that run deeper than names or even blood. Up here Iain, we have a life. We have a connection to the land."

He opened his eyes again.

"I must warn you though bud, this isn't for everyone. Some people like the idea of starting over in the middle of nowhere but they can't hack the reality. We only invite people into the Hand who're fully committed. Committed for the long haul. The people who come in must work the land, develop spiritually and emotionally in harmony with the rest of the community. They can't just turn tail and run when they realise we don't do five-minute microwave meals, Facebook feeds or Netflix and chill. We ask only one thing before entry is permitted. That you cast off the baggage from your previous life. Nothing of that can come with you. We can't evolve until we peel off our scars. Until we're clean. Do you understand what I'm saying?"

Iain didn't understand. But he nodded anyway.

"Yes."

"Iain – you've got baggage," Harris said. "It's in your eyes. You've got more baggage than most."

"I know."

"Are you willing to do whatever it takes? Are you willing to cleanse yourself?"

"Yes."

Harris stood up, removed his black coat from the back of the chair. He threaded his arms through the sleeves. Then he walked around the table, stopping beside Iain's chair. He put his hands on Iain's shoulder and began to massage them softly.

Iain's body seized up. But he didn't protest.

"Jay Green," Harris said. "Davie Muir. Where are they now?"

"They're not my friends anymore," Iain said. "I don't know where they are. I don't care either."

Harris laughed. Alison and Jonas joined in, as if this was a signal.

"You *do* care," Harris said. "That's why you've been carrying them around inside you for years. Their faces. Their names. Those two men – they're your baggage. They're weighing you down, bud."

Iain glanced at the ceilidh band setting up in the corner of the bar. Old hippie-type men were busy tuning guitars and banjos. Fiddles were removed from their cases. Looked like a good gig coming up.

"What does all this mean?" Iain asked.

Harris took his hands off Iain's shoulders. Stepped to the side so Iain could see his face.

"Iain, I'd like to invite you to the village tomorrow. Alison and Jonas will come pick you up in the morning. Spend a few days with us before you go back to Glasgow, aye? We'll talk some more after you experience our community for yourself."

"Okay," Iain said, his heart fluttering with excitement. "Thanks."

He looked at Alison. She was watching him from across the table, her face frozen in a beatific smile.

"It's a big commitment," she said, reaching over and taking his hand. "But Iain, I know you've got what it takes to join us. I know you can do it."

17

IAIN

Iain couldn't stop laughing.

He was bent over double like he'd been back in the mid-nineties when he, Jay and Davie had taken their first double dose of acid together. During that nine-hour laughing fit, they'd laughed at everything. Strangers. The toppings on the pizza they'd ordered. It was non-stop and then, just as now, Iain couldn't keep a lid on it.

This was *his* time. Finally, after all these years of being sealed up inside himself, he was free.

He stabbed a finger at his old friends as he laughed. Look at them, Iain thought. They look so stupid. Trapped outside the cabin with their dumb, shocked expressions, still trying to process the truth. Did they understand yet? Look at Jay, his dreamy brown eyes filling up with panic. Ha-ha! And Davie, his fancy-pants wheelchair going nowhere fast. Now he's all helpless and vulnerable. Not so cool now, are you Davie boy? Look at you. You look like a shell-shocked, crippled war veteran that still thinks he's got legs.

Iain couldn't blame them for being confused. He hadn't known what was going on at first either. It's not like Harris or anyone had warned him about the kidnapping. Iain thought he'd been abducted by a bunch of loonies. Things only made sense when Harris had turned up at the cabin door dressed as a policeman. That was Iain's big lightbulb moment. After that, it was clear. The triple kidnapping. The note. The killer.

It was all for Iain.

Tonight, was his cleansing. It was his initiation into the Hand of Glory – that wonderful community that thrived in the heartlands, away from prying eyes and an overreliance on machinery and superficial distraction. They *wanted* him. They'd set this whole thing up for him and this was to be the moment of truth. The moment he left his old life behind and walked into the new one.

Iain Lewis was the killer. The confession was his to make. And yet after figuring out the truth, Iain hadn't rushed outside to make that confession. Sure, he'd been shot in the leg by Harris (a test of course) but wasn't there a part of him that wanted to stay in the cabin? That wanted to spend more time with Jay and Davie?

He shook his head, disagreeing with his inner voice.

No.

Jay and Davie didn't understand. After all the hours they'd spent with Iain in the cabin, they still didn't acknowledge what they'd done to him when they dropped him. This was *their* fault. They'd made him like this. So be it. Iain's mind was clear. The snow was falling and it was going to be a wild, beautiful night in the Highlands. A perfect night to be reborn. After the cleansing, he'd already decided to ask Harris for a new name. He wanted a new identity. And then he'd change his hair, maybe even dye it, and then he'd get back in shape and start over with Alison by his side. It wasn't too late to be a dad. To get married.

Sometimes, the excitement of it all was too much.

He *would* kill them today. And in the process, he'd be killing Iain Lewis too. The man that nobody wanted.

"Why didn't you just check in once in a while?" he yelled. Iain wasn't laughing anymore. His voice cracked, echoing across the vast landscape and disappearing into a white abyss. "You didn't even think to do that? To look me up, see if I was okay? Not once in twenty years? You never thought about *me*?"

He continued to stab a finger at them.

"Friends don't do that to friends."

Jay crept forward, hands up in the air. His bottom lip trembled and he looked so scared that Iain wanted to laugh, but the well was dry.

"Iain, mate."

Iain shook his head. "Don't call me *mate*."

"Think about what's going on here right now," Jay said, nervously glancing at Harris and the rest of the Hand. "Will you please talk to me? I'm listening. Davie and me, we're both listening and..."

"Fuck off!" Iain snapped, his lips curling into a snarl. "You don't give a flying fuck about me so don't insult my intelligence by pretending to be my friend."

All the hatred, clogged up inside Iain like plaque in the arteries, was finally moving. He was exhausted and elated. This was the process of Iain Lewis dying, but it would be okay. After the cleansing, he'd no longer be the pathetic loser who could only feel something by watching other people's reunions in the airport, sucking out second-hand happiness like a leech.

"I'm going to kill you," he said. "I'm going to kill both of you."

Jay shook his head. Davie, his wheelchair stuck in the snow, watched in stunned silence.

Alison appeared at Iain's side, putting her arm around his shoulder. Iain loved her for that gesture of support when he needed it most. The Hand was his family now. These were his friends, his purpose, his everything. Could Alison ever love him as much as he loved her? Maybe after he'd proved himself to her and to the Hand. After he'd shown Harris how committed he was to their way of life, to their rejection of modernity and its glittery, empty web.

"They've brainwashed you," Jay said. "That woman. That man – they've brainwashed you Iain. You hear me mate? It's a cult – it's a fucking cult."

Jay glanced at Davie for help. Davie stared at Iain, at Alison, at the Hand. But he said nothing.

"Killing us won't make the pain go away," Jay called out. "It'll get worse, I guarantee it man. This, whatever this is, it isn't the answer. Please listen to me. Please think clearly about this. It's murder Iain."

Jay walked towards Iain. As he did, two burly figures in long coats appeared on either side of him. It was as if they'd been waiting in the shadows and when he moved, they grabbed an arm each, bringing Jay's progress to a halt.

Iain applauded the intervention.

Jay's eyes were wild with panic. He struggled to break free but the two heavies were far too strong for him. He was going nowhere.

Iain giggled, pointed at Jay. *You look silly*.

"I've got a baby on the way!" Jay screamed, loud enough for everyone to hear. "Please! Doesn't that mean anything to anyone? You'll go to prison Iain. These crazy bastards don't know how this'll end but I do. I do! This won't make your life any better. Are you listening to me for God's sake?"

Harris walked past Iain and Alison, approaching the cabin with a blank expression. About five of his followers strolled alongside Harris, each one with a plastic petrol container in hand.

Iain could hear the liquid swirling around inside the containers.

"It's nearly time," he said.

Jay's eyes bulged in terror as he processed what was happening. Davie, that bastard, was giving Iain nothing. No crying, no begging, nothing. At least, not yet.

Some of Harris's men tipped the fuel out around the cabin exterior. Others went inside to soak the hallway.

"As far as the police are concerned," Harris said to Jay and Davie, "Iain Lewis was kidnapped at Glasgow Airport yesterday. He's a victim of a terrible revenge crime, along with Jason Green and David Muir, the other two Lads, kidnapped on the eve of their school reunion. Most likely, the authorities will agree that it has something to do with school. With a disgruntled former victim. Wouldn't you agree?"

"You're fucking crazy," Jay said. "You're all fucking crazy!"

Harris smiled. "No one will ever find Iain. We're a remote community and it's our choice to remain hidden. So please, don't worry about him going to jail."

Harris took a step backwards, then gazed up at the darkening sky.

"Nice night for a fire."

18

JAY

Jay had never known fear in all of his forty-four years.

Not real fear, not like this. He'd been in plenty of sticky situations, some far worse than others, but nothing he'd experienced in the past came close to this. Real fear was watching strangers pouring petrol in and around the cabin. Real fear was knowing what came next. It was the thought of never seeing Rachel again. It was Rachel never finding out what happened, never even getting close to the truth, and all the nightmares she'd have trying to fill in the blanks. Real fear, it was the thought of never seeing or holding their precious child, not even once.

He had to reach Iain. Pull Iain back.

It was up to him alone to avert this disaster. Davie was a broken wreck, sitting in his wheelchair and staring at the cult members without a hint of emotion. Waiting to die. What was wrong with him? Why wasn't he fighting to go back to his family? Was the shock of Iain's betrayal too much?

"Iain," Jay said. There were still two heavies standing on either side of him. Long haired, bearded and with enough muscle between them to turn Jay's head into mush if he so much as put a foot wrong. "This is all my fault and I'm sorry. I'm *so* sorry. I treated you badly, but we can work through this. We *can*. Call this off and we'll sit down and talk, just the three of us. Just the three of us Iain, like it used to be in the old days. It's our business and it doesn't concern these people. What do you say?"

Iain's arm was wrapped around the red-haired woman's shoulder. What did he call her again? Alison?

"Please," Jay said. He could hear the sloshing of the petrol being tipped out behind him. "You've made your point, your friends have made their point and we'll say nothing more about this. Okay? We'll say nothing. Will we Davie?"

Davie didn't answer.

"Fucking hell Davie!" Jay screamed. He didn't recognise his voice anymore. "Will you say something for Christ's sake? Help me out man. Don't you see what's happening? They're going to burn us alive in there. *Both* of us."

Davie blinked, as if waking from a dream. He looked like he was about to say something, but then the sound of foot-steps got in his way.

It was Mutton Chops. He walked towards Jay, the rifle hanging at his side. He used the gun like a walking stick, his fingers gripped tight over the barrel as he worked his way through the snow. Behind him, Alison whispered something into Iain's ear. Whatever she said, it made Iain laugh. They followed Mutton Chops towards the cabin. Towards Jay and Davie.

Jay's flimsy voice continued to betray him. "You won't get away with this, I swear to God."

Mutton Chops stabbed the butt of his rifle into the snow and came to a stop. "Relax Jay. Everything's okay."

"Okay? You think burning two people alive is okay?"

Mutton Chops pointed to the men with the petrol cans. "What? You really think we'd burn down a perfectly good cabin for the likes of you?"

Jay shook his head in disbelief. "What?"

"It's just another one of my little pranks," Mutton Chops said, winking at Jay. "Just a joke bud. It's only water they're pouring out. It's the snow that we melted earlier while we were waiting for you guys to come out."

"A joke?" Jay screamed. His face was burning hot. He wanted nothing more than to take a swing at this clown but he knew the two heavies beside him would separate Jay from consciousness before he got the chance to make a fist. "You think this is funny? Do you actually think this is fucking funny?"

Iain laughed. Sounded like a tortured bird screaming in pain.

"You're funny Jay," he said, tears streaming down his eyes. "I think *you're* funny man."

Iain pointed to the cabin.

"You're going to burn for what you did to me. You and Davie, you're…"

"No," Mutton Chops said, cutting Iain off. He glanced over his shoulder at Iain and Alison. "No they're not."

Iain's face wrinkled up in taut confusion.

"What are you talking about?" he said, storming over to Mutton Chops. "You were kidding around with him just there, weren't you? Water – ha, good one. That *is* real petrol they're pouring out inside the cabin. You're just pretending it isn't, eh?"

Mutton Chops shook his head. "It's only water."

Iain's mouth opened and closed like a dying goldfish. "I don't understand. I thought...this is my cleansing. We were going to...this is *my* cleansing, isn't it?"

Mutton Chops spoke in a calm voice. "You won't be killing anyone tonight."

Iain's jaw dropped. "Harris?"

Jay's ears pricked up. Harris, he thought. So that was Mutton Chops' real name.

Harris.

Why was Harris staring at Jay with such fierce intensity, ignoring the desperate pleas of Iain behind him?

"What are you talking about?" Iain's outraged voice yelled. He grabbed Harris by the shoulder and spun him around. Both men stumbled, nearly falling over. They righted themselves and when the heavies standing beside Jay turned towards Iain, Harris waved them off.

Iain and Harris faced one another, their noses almost touching.

"Why am I here?" Iain said, his face contorted with rage. He pointed at Jay and Davie. "They're mine. *My* cleansing, it's my cleansing. This, all of this, was for me, wasn't it?"

Iain's breath was a jet of white mist. "I'm ready. Give me the matches and I'll do it. I'll burn that shithole down with them in it."

The howling wind whipped the falling snow into a frenzy, blowing it in different directions.

Harris shook his head. "Iain, I'm sorry."

"Eh?"

"You've been slightly misled."

"What do you mean?"

"This is *my* cleansing. Not yours."

Jay watched these events unfold in a growing state of confusion. He didn't have the first clue as to what was going on anymore and wondered if this was all a chaotic dream. He pinched the frozen skin on the back of his hand, but didn't wake up in bed beside a softly-snoring Rachel.

Iain blinked furiously. "What? What do you mean it's *your* cleansing?"

Harris glanced at Jay, his face white like a ghoul. He turned towards the cabin, spoke with his back to Iain.

"This was never about you Iain. I realised within about five minutes of meeting you that you wouldn't be a good fit for our community."

Iain stared at Harris's back, his face wrinkled up in confusion. Slowly, he turned around to face Alison. He reached for her. Opened his arms, seeking another embrace.

"Alison..."

The red-haired woman glided across the snow like an apparition, her hair flapping in the wind and the snow swirling all around her.

"Alison," Iain said in a meek voice. "It's another joke, isn't it?"

Alison looked at Iain like he was a dying bird she'd found at the side of the road. The pity didn't last. "I'm sorry Iain. I tried to speak up for you but when Harris found out about..."

She pointed the rifle at Iain.

"It's okay – you won't feel a thing anymore."

"Alison?"

Jay's body flinched at the solitary crack of gunfire. He let out a loud gasp. He saw an explosion of red mist as the bullet pierced Iain's skull. Iain's body stiffened and toppled backwards onto the snow with a soft thud. Then he was still, arms extended at the sides like he was making a snow angel.

"Jesus Christ," Jay said. His body shook violently. He looked at the body, waiting for Iain to get back up. Waiting for a round of applause, this time in appreciation of another sick joke.

He clamped a hand over his mouth. This was it – they were going to kill him and there was no way around that now, not after what he'd just witnessed. They'd just killed Iain, right in front of him. He was going to be shot in the head and dumped in an unmarked grave, here in a place where there were no people. The snow and ice would thaw. Animals would scavenge on his remains. And that would be the end of it.

Jay heard Davie's voice at long last – it was a whisper.

"Iain. I'm sorry."

Harris glanced at the body in the snow. He nodded in Alison's direction before turning his attention back to Jay.

"Nice guy, but he had some issues."

Jay's heart was thumping against his ribcage. "I won't tell anyone. Swear to God, I won't talk."

Harris took a step closer to Jay, using his rifle as a walking stick again. "You don't recognise me?"

He thrust his head forward, inviting Jay to take a look. "You really don't remember me, do you Jay? And yet, I remember you so well. I have to say, you look pretty good man, all things considered."

"You just fucking killed a man in cold blood," Jay said. "Tell me who you are."

Harris wagged his finger in the air. Made a tut-tutting noise.

"Don't act like you cared about Iain. It insults my intelligence. He told me all about you guys, about how you turned your backs on him after school. I got the whole story and I'm sure you did too in there. Hey, at least now he'll never bring that up again."

Jay studied the man's face. He was searching for something familiar in the eyes, in the lines, in the microscopic mannerisms that might leak information. He concentrated so hard it felt like his skull would crack.

"Who are you?"

"I'm not surprised you don't remember me," Harris said. "I've gained some weight since the last time we met. Good thing too because back then, I was a skeleton. Back then, when we last saw one another, I was dying."

Jay felt like he was swaying from side to side. His thoughts blown around by confusion like the snowflakes at the mercy of the wind. "What?"

"Talking about the old days bud."

Jay nodded. "Were you in the same year as us? Did I bully you? Is that what this is?"

"No," Harris said. "Let's get this straight – I did go to Strathmore but I was two years older than you and your pals. We didn't mix, not at school anyway. I'm not a victim of your bullying come back to haunt you. You should be so lucky."

Jay felt numb, both with cold and terror.

"Who are you then?"

"The bullying angle is a great one though," Harris said, avoiding the question. "Makes for a great story and that's why we staged three kidnappings. I'm willing to bet that some of your former classmates will be getting a knock on the door from the police in the morning. Poor bastards, it's comical. A vengeance mob rising up against the school bullies twenty-five years later. But it'll keep the police busy for a while. Don't you think?"

Harris pointed to Iain's body.

"Poor Iain. He really *was* all set to burn you alive tonight. He thought it was his cleansing when really, it was mine."

"Cleansing?"

"It's a purification ritual of sorts. I believe that cleansing ourselves of past burdens, past resentments, past negativity, is essential for moving on. Succumb to nature's urge and do the terrible deed. Kill the past. Give birth to the future. Quite literally."

Jay looked at Iain. The snow had covered most of his face already. An instant burial, courtesy of Mother Nature.

"You're a murderer."

"Imagine my surprise," Harris said, "when I found out that Alison's latest recruit was Iain Lewis from Strathmore Academy. Incredible! I thought I was going to The Old Tavern for a routine recruitment meeting. And there he was, sitting right in front of me. One of the Lads. I remembered the Lads alright, one in particular. And once you were back in my head Jason Green, I couldn't stop thinking about you."

"I'm getting sick of this," Jay said. "Just fucking tell me, *Harris*. Tell me or shoot me in the head and spare me your bullshit."

Harris's eyes blackened, the irises rotting like dead flowers. "Okay Jay. Back in the mid-nineties, when we knew each other, I had a nickname."

Jay shrugged. "And?"

"Back then," Harris said, "when I was a heroin addict, people called me Beano."

That did it. Jay's legs immediately gave out on him. He fell onto his knees, then collapsed onto his backside. "No... please, no. No, no, no, no...""

He looked up at Harris. Saw a bearded devil leaning over him, the red-haired witch standing at his side.

"You're lying," Jay said. "Beano died of a heroin overdose. Back in 1997, he died."

Harris shook his head. "That's the story that went around town, isn't it? But that's not what happened. I was alive when I was dumped at the side of the road that day. Dying from a heroin overdose. I was alive in the ambulance. Still alive in the hospital. And somehow, even though I would have been quite happy to die that day, I pulled through. The reaper moved on, I lived. And kept living up to this day."

"Beano died," Jay said, unable to look the man in the face. He was scared that Beano *was* in alive in Harris. In Mutton Chops. "If you...if *Beano* didn't die, why did I never see him around town again?"

"My mother was so freaked out." Harris said, "that she'd moved our things out of our house before I even woke up in hospital. We were gone. I protested, but I didn't have a leg to stand on. Didn't have much strength to fight her either, not for a long time. Her reasoning was that she didn't want any of my old acquaintances dragging me down again. I didn't like it, but I can't say I blame her. That town, *our* town, wasn't good for me."

He walked over and whispered in Jay's ear.

"Everyone thought I was dead, eh? Pretty crazy, but that wasn't even the worst rumour that went around town in the aftermath of my OD, was it?"

Jay closed his eyes and shook his head.

"There was another one," Beano said.

"No."

"The second rumour," Harris said, "the *worst* rumour was that Terry Braithwaite, my very best friend in the world, dumped me at the side of the road after he found me OD'ing on the couch. They said he left me for dead. Even today, I'll bet that's still the story going around town. Right? Terry Braithwaite, oh you mean the fucked-up junkie that dumped his dying pal on the street?"

Jay shivered. But he couldn't feel the cold anymore.

"Please…"

Harris held up a hand, indicating that he wasn't finished.

"I might have been strung out of my mind that day. But I remember. I've always remembered and now it's time to right the wrongs of history. Because it wasn't poor old Terry that left me to die on the side of the road. Was it, Jay?"

19

JAY

October 12ᵗʰ, 1997

Jay Green couldn't believe what he was seeing. He'd always known this sort of thing could happen, especially since he'd started hanging around with these skagheads after leaving school. But he never thought it *would* happen.

Beano was overdosing. This was a real-life heroin overdose, happening right in front of Jay's eyes.

Most likely, Beano was dying.

"Get up" Jay said, standing beside the couch where Beano was foaming at the mouth. He was flat on his back, his arms and legs limp, eyes half-open, his skin a horrible shade of yellow around the face and neck.

He looked like a wax dummy that had been left to rot in the sun.

Jay grabbed Beano's pencil-thin arm, shook it. He hit his shoulder, yelling at the top of his voice to try and summon Beano back from the abyss.

"For fuck's sake man, get up!"

Both Beano and Terry were out of their skulls, but Beano was in far worse shape than his best mate. Terry was upstairs, sprawled out on the queen-sized bed, semi-conscious, surrounded by several Fender Strats, a copy of *Kerrang* magazine, a Keith Moon biography and the scent of stale smoke that seemed to have always lived in the walls in Terry's house. He was in a hazy trance-like state, but he didn't seem to be in any serious danger.

Not like Beano.

It was bad timing – the worst timing. Jay had only shown up at Terry's house to poke his head through the door and collect his weed money for the month. He'd found the front door ajar, which was strange, and so Jay had walked in apprehensively. It was quiet too, apart from The Verve's *Urban Hymns* album playing on the stereo. The house stank like it always did, secreting a cocktail of beer and smoke, as well as the ghastly body odour that let everyone know Beano was in the house.

Jay thought Beano was asleep at first. But a vague sense of unease prompted him to take a closer look.

When he realised what was happening, Jay sprinted upstairs and discovered Terry, semi-conscious on the bed. Terry was too far gone to be useful. He didn't acknowledge Jay or respond in any way to what Jay was telling him about Beano OD'ing in the living room. Jay cursed, then abandoned his efforts to rouse Terry. It was clear that Terry didn't have the faintest clue what was going on around him. He didn't seem to realise that Jay was even there.

Jay ran downstairs in a panic, unsure of what to do next.

"Beano!" Jay said, leaning over the couch. He slapped Beano on the face. The slaps were gentle at first but hardened as the junkie remained unresponsive. "Can you hear me? Wake up man for fuck's sake."

It was too late.

Beano was going to die.

Jay backed away from the couch, his mouth hanging open. He spun around to get Beano out of his sight. As he did so, he caught sight of his reflection in an oval-shaped mirror hanging over the mantelpiece. Oh God, he thought. I'm even starting to resemble them. And he was. More and more, Jay was transforming from a handsome young man into another version of Terry and Beano. The long, greasy hair that hadn't been washed in weeks. Patched denims. The bloodshot eyes. Pasty skin.

"What are you doing here?" he said. "Why are you here? You want to end up like this? Like them?"

Terry had inherited the detached house after his mother's death from breast cancer three years ago. Since then, the well-kept property had deteriorated into a typical junkie den. The square patch of grass out front, once tended to perfection by Mrs Braithwaite, hadn't been cut in months. Inside, the house was a tip. The furniture was old and crusty, covered in empty Rizla packets and there were abandoned beer cans on the floor, the window-ledge and even surrounding the toilet. The coffee table beside the couch was covered in drug paraphernalia: needles, spoons, cotton balls, lighters and the shoelace that Terry and Beano used to tie off their limbs and make the veins pop.

Jay wasn't supposed to be here.

He'd ignored that nagging voice in his head (it sounded a lot like his mum's voice) that told him he was in over his head with these people. Why had he gotten mixed up with Terry, Beano and their druggie mates in the first place? That was easy. Jay made good money selling Terry's weed to the locals. There were plenty of customers around and they were only too willing to pay a solid price. Besides that, Terry was a pretty chilled out guy and Jay liked him. They shared a love of good music and Jay had even started learning the guitar so he could keep up with the impromptu stoner jams at Terry's all-night parties. Only that morning, he'd been working on the intro to 'Wish You Were Here' by Pink Floyd.

He almost had it down too.

Dealing hadn't been a long-term career plan. At first, he'd planned to do it for a few months, then move on when he found something better. Something that actually inspired him. But a few months had turned into a year. That year was now two years. Jay was pissing his life away, too lazy and apathetic to change, and now he'd walked into the middle of a fatal drugs overdose. Talk about a wake-up call.

He winced as Beano made a gargling noise on the couch.

Jay stood there, feeling helpless. What was he was supposed to do with this guy? He was twenty years old and it felt like his future was hanging in the balance. He didn't know first aid and he was too frightened to call an ambulance because he thought they'd be able to track him down after the call.

He could *not* be here. His business with Terry was a well-kept secret for the most part, at least where his parents were concerned.

Richard Ashcroft's soulful voice floated out of the stereo speakers, telling the listener that the drugs don't work.

Looking at Beano, that was hard to believe.

He had to do something.

"Alright," he said, hurrying over and dropping onto his knees beside the couch. How old was Beano anyway? Twenty-one? Twenty-two? The man was a walking skeleton. His arms and legs, as taut as piano wire. There were no reserves in that flimsy excuse of a body, which meant if he didn't have an iron will to live, there was no way he was going to pull through.

"Beano…"

What was his real name anyway? Jay had only ever known him as Beano, as Terry's best mate. He was just a boy who'd fucked up. The biggest junkie in town, slightly eccentric, with bizarre ideas about revolution, about creating utopian societies and how to get rid of the Royal Family (who by the way were lizards) and much, much more. But still, he was a human being. He didn't deserve to die so young.

"C'mon."

Jay wrapped an arm around Beano's shoulder and locked in a tight grip. With a rallying cry, he got him up to his feet. He'd expected something heavier to come off the couch but Beano was as light as a children's ragdoll.

"Hang on Beano," Jay said, adjusting his grip, relocating his arm down to Beano's waist. Once he had him, Jay dragged Beano through the hallway, passing a stack of guitar cases piled up against the wall. Those cases were a reminder of better times.

Jay nudged the front door open with his shoe. He looked outside, half-expecting to find the police or a mob of locals waiting for him, armed with torches and pitchforks and murderous threats. *Come out junkies! Come out with your hands above your head!* It was no secret the locals couldn't stand Terry and what he'd done with his mother's house since her death. With his druggie mates and druggie parties, he'd brought down the tone of the respectable cul-de-sac.

Jay thought about the nearby church, St Mary's. He wondered if he could get Beano over there, knock on the door and then make a run for it?

No. How many CCTV cameras would spot him on the

way? Besides, his parents knew the minister. If the minister saw Jay, he was in deep shit.

Jay glanced up and down the tiny street. He could only hope there were no surveillance cameras installed around here or he was already in deep shit.

God, what a mess.

He was halfway down the path, dragging Beano like a sack. The man was so *light*. It was like he was made of tracing paper.

Jay was done with this shit. This lifestyle, it was over, starting today. He couldn't be associated with these people anymore. He was scared stiff, fucking petrified of ending up like these losers with their scruffy Iron Maiden image, long hair, pasty complexions and faded denims. They could smoke, snort or inject themselves into oblivion as far as Jay was concerned.

"Think," he said. "What do I do with him? What do I do?"

But Jay had known from the start what he was going to do. Deep down. Even after he'd gone through the pretence of getting Beano off the couch, acting like a concerned friend and hauling him outside, Jay knew what he was going to do.

He was going to save his own skin.

No one knew he was at the house. No one except Terry but Terry was doing a loop the loop rollercoaster ride in heroin Disneyland right now and he wouldn't remember a thing about Jay standing over the bed. If he did, Terry would think it nothing but a dream.

Survival of the fittest. And of the smartest.

Jay would treat this as a valuable life lesson, a crucial step in his personal evolution. It was a memory to file away, to keep to himself for the rest of his life. And if he ever thought of it again, he'd remember it as a kick in the arse that propelled him to better things. He'd remember it as other people would remember it – as a terrible, but inevitable tragedy that was bound to happen sooner or later.

Under his denim jacket, Jay wore a Top Shop hoodie. He grabbed the hood and pulled it over his head, tucking his long, greasy hair in at the sides. *Fuck, fuck, fuck!* He was already at the end of the path and now he steered the floppy-limbed Beano through the open gate, coming to a stop at the side of the road. Jay lowered Beano onto the pavement, resting his back against the red brick wall outside the Braithwaite house. Beano tilted a little to the side, the broken doll falling back to earth.

Jay backed away.

It was a quiet road, but someone would show up and find Beano sooner or later. He was clearly visible to anyone who turned into the street from the main road. How long before the commuters started coming home? An hour or two? Someone would find him, Jay repeated silently to himself. They'd find him and drive him to the hospital.

He couldn't be here.

"That's the best I can do mate," Jay whispered, his eyes skimming over the windows of the nearby houses. No one was watching. No curious, disapproving faces peeked out from behind the neighbourhood curtains.

Jay turned and broke into a sprint. To the main road, to home. He was a different man now and he'd prove it by getting rid of his drug stash when he got home. Not the money, he'd use that up, but the drugs were gone. That was the first thing he was going to do. Then he'd get rid of the shitty clothes too.

Maybe he'd get his hair cut tomorrow. His parents would appreciate that.

20

DAVIE

Davie sat in his chair, numb.

Watching.

The stillness of Iain's corpse was a resounding statement – it was the official end of the Lads, not the start of another twenty-year holiday from one another, but the end. Davie could still hear the dead man's hysterical laughter ringing in his ears, an endless echo from the snowy grave. Before he died, Iain had been on the brink of burning them alive. And he'd been laughing about it. Such was Iain's belief in Jay and Davie's betrayal that for him, the burning wasn't a hideous crime, but justice. Then came the gunshot. The red-haired woman's betrayal. And now Iain as a snow angel, watched over by a silent huddle of masks.

Then came the revelation about Beano. And then Jay, on his hands and knees, begging for his life.

It was only a matter of time, Davie thought. Soon he and Jay would be as dead as Iain. There was no way out of this and yet there it was – this strange sense of detachment that had followed Davie out of the cabin like a shadow. As if all this was happening to someone else. He should have been hysterical like Jay but he couldn't do it. He had something to live for, didn't he? He had a family. But Davie deserved to die and he couldn't shake off the feeling that it was his time. Hadn't he always suspected that it wouldn't end well for him. He'd never envisioned an end quite like this one, but it was never going to be pretty. The Lads didn't deserve pretty, and Davie least of all.

He watched as Mutton Chops, aka Beano, aka Harris, stood over the kneeling Jay. Jay's head was lowered, awaiting the executioner's axe.

Harris stabbed the butt of the rifle at Jay's face, missing by inches. "Say it, Jay. After all this time I want to hear you say it."

Jay sobbed. "It wasn't Terry who left you for dead."

"Who was it?"

"Me. It was me."

Davie could hardly recognise Jay's voice anymore. The bluster was gone, the swagger and sureness gone. His begging, pleading tone was childlike. Davie recalled the day of the lorry incident. The chorus of desperation that had seeped up off the street like morning mist after the lorry had come to a stop. All those people hurt and bleeding on the ground, begging for help.

Begging for their lives, like Jay.

"Terry didn't know," Harris said, snarling, raising a clenched fist in the air above Jay's head. "He believed that he was responsible – that he'd dragged me down the path and dumped me on the side of the street. He loved me man. I was his best friend. I was in recovery – I never got a chance to tell him what really happened before he...."

Jay clasped his hands together. "I didn't start those

rumours."

"You didn't stop them," Harris said. "Did you? Didn't even think to make an anonymous call to Terry, telling him that someone else was involved. Give him some hope for God's sake. And that's why you're here. You let my friend die. You were the only one who knew the truth and even when you heard the rumours, when you heard people blaming Terry and giving him all kinds of shit, you kept it to yourself. You selfish fucking coward."

"Let it out Harris," Alison said. She stood in between Harris and the silent horde of masks. "Let it all out."

Harris held the rifle like a baseball bat. Fingers tightly wrapped around the barrel. It was inches away from coming down on Jay's head.

"No," Davie whispered.

"I remember," Harris said, tears running down his face. "I remember everything. I remember your face coming through the fog that day, as if heaven sent. I couldn't talk, but I could think. Jay's found me, I thought. Help's on its way. See, I didn't want to die Jay. I was twenty-two years old, scared shitless of dying. I hadn't done anything with my life."

Jay wept into his palms. His hands were red with the cold. "I was scared. I was so scared and I..."

Harris lowered the rifle. "You were scared? How do you think I felt?"

Davie glanced at Iain's body. He couldn't stop looking at it. The lifeless eyes were open, the shock of Alison's violent rejection carved onto his ghoulish features.

"After Terry slit his wrists," Harris said to Jay, "I didn't think about revenge. I was too busy getting my shit together and so I didn't spend my life sulking like poor Iain here. I blamed myself for my problems and when I moved to Edinburgh with my family, I tried to get on with things. To recover what my therapist deemed a normal life."

He chuckled, replaying some old memory in his head.

"The drugs were gone but I was still the same restless soul I'd always been. My family tried to change that. They wanted me to go to night school. Go to college. And at the end of all that, a nine-to-five job and a nice girlfriend and supposedly, they said, that was happiness. I fought a lot with my mum about that. About what happiness was. Day after day we fought and, in the end, I left home without saying goodbye. This was about a year and a half after the overdose. But I never used heroin again. I wasn't looking for a high you see, I was looking for something more. Something deeper."

Jay's black hair was peppered with snowflakes. He apologised over and over again, bowing at the feet of the man in front of him.

"I built the Hand," Harris said. "Took me long enough but eventually I put together a self-reliant community, far from the noise of modernity. For the first time in my life, I was happy. The past was behind me. That overdose, it was someone else's bad dream. It was Beano's nightmare, not mine. And then one night in Gairloch, Iain walked into the Old Tavern and...well, here we are. Turns out the past isn't behind me, not yet."

Jay worked his way back to his feet. He glanced warily at the two men flanking him. "How can I make it up to you? There must be something – something you need that I can get. For you, for the community. Please...Rachel's pregnant. The baby needs a father. Don't punish them for the mistakes of a frightened boy, please."

Davie toggled the joystick on his chair. He had to at least try and stop this. But the snow was getting deeper and the chair struggled to move. He turned the power off and disengaged the yellow freewheel levers. It wasn't much better on manual.

"Fuck."

He called over, but they weren't listening to him. It was as if he didn't exist.

Harris pointed to the rest of the masks, including Alison.

"How can I lead these people forward with my head stuck in the past? How can I propose a cleansing for anyone else when it turns out I'm not clean? That's no good Jay. You understand, I have to fix that."

Jay was still sobbing uncontrollably. "Harris. Tell me. What can I do?"

Davie saw that Jay was inching closer to Harris. Shuffling forward. He didn't know if Jay realised what he was doing or how threatening it looked. He wanted to call out, to tell Jay to stop but it was too late. The heavies grabbed him, taking an arm each. They twisted both limbs behind Jay's back and Jay, who was taken by surprise, screamed like a wild animal caught in a steel-jaw trap.

Davie winced, feeling sympathy pains in his own arms. He watched his friend wriggle in their joint grip. But it was no use. Jay was doomed, like a worm trapped in a giant beak.

Davie thought about Elena and the kids, six hundred miles south of here in London. How he'd miss them. How he already missed them so bad. Davie cursed himself for not telling his family that he loved them before he'd steered the chair up the platform ramp yesterday at Euston. Three little words, he didn't say them enough. But then again, didn't everyone say that?

Fuck. Even his regret was a cliché.

Harris's goons put more pressure on Jay's arms. How they hadn't snapped yet was a miracle in defiance of physics. Jay's body spasmed in response to the pressure. He tried to twist the arms back in the opposite direction, to manoeuvre a release, but they had him locked up good.

"Cuff him," Harris said.

"No!" Jay screamed.

Davie saw the glint of metal in one of the big men's hands. There was a sharp click as the handcuffs snapped shut around Jay's wrists. His arms were now trapped behind his back.

Jay thrashed and kicked at his captors. Expending what little energy he had left in a frantic bid for escape. "Davie! Help me. Davie, please help me!"

Davie reached for his old friend.

"Stop fighting Jay."

Harris dusted the snow off the arms of his coat. Then he slowly began to circle Jay, his black mutton chop beard, piercing eyes and snarl giving him a wolf-like appearance.

"You know," he said, "approximately one hundred and sixty thousand people die every day across the world. Mostly in places with obscene populations like China and India. But they die here too. It could have been me twenty-two years ago, lying on the side of the street that day outside Terry's house. That could have been my time. One less junkie in the world. Most people would have celebrated. Even you, a so-called mate, didn't call an ambulance, did you Jay?"

"Beano," Jay cried out. "Please..."

"But I lived. Isn't that incredible? I lived and in the same minute that fate turned in my favour, one hundred and fourteen people across the world dropped dead. One hundred and fourteen people, that's how many die every minute. Do you know how many minutes there are in a day? One thousand, four hundred and forty. There I was, shooting skag in my veins, giving Mother Nature every reason to hit the ejector seat button. And yet, I lived. Isn't life bizarre?"

Harris laughed, his breath shooting out like mist.

"Isn't this better than a school reunion?"

"I can give you money," Jay said, his voice hoarse and fading. "I've got money put away – lots of it. It's all yours. Whatever you want. I can finance your community, the Hand, on an ongoing basis, eh? How about that? You'll need money to get things, to bring things up here and make it flourish long term. I can help. I've got tons of connections. Just please don't kill me. Please."

Harris closed his eyes. "Let me tell you what's going to happen to you Jay."

He pointed to the distant, pink-hued horizon. Beyond the loch, to the monstrous, white tipped hills receding behind the mist.

"We're going to take you over there. Up to the hills, or at least as far as we can go in these conditions before the roads become impenetrable. You'll be stripped naked, cuffed on the legs as well as the wrists. After that, you'll be abandoned. We'll leave you up there with no clothes, no food, no shelter. No hope of rescue."

Davie listened to Jay's shrill screams as his fate was laid bare. He tried to move the chair again, to get over there, but the snow held him back.

"Abandoned," Harris said. "Just like you abandoned me. And more importantly, like you abandoned Terry."

Harris put his arm around Alison. They were still

standing over the hump that was Iain's snow-covered body. Acting as if it wasn't there.

"You'll have some time before you freeze to death," Harris said to Jay. "Up there, you know? Time to think about your woman and child. Time to imagine what the child will look like in one year, two years, three years and so on. Whether it'll take after you. I'm sorry that Rachel will suffer but in time she'll move on. Terry's family moved on, eventually. Did you know that he had a young daughter, Jay?"

Jay was spent. He could barely speak through his constant sobbing.

"Please..."

"Maybe when you're alone out there," Harris said, "frozen solid and unable to feel anything anymore. Maybe you'll see Terry in the mist. Maybe he'll come for you. Oh, he won't be smiling Jay. He will *not* be smiling."

"Please. Don't do this."

Harris looked at Alison, gave a casual shrug. "Rachel's a very attractive woman. Won't take long for her to find someone else to share her bed. And your child, well they'll grow up calling someone else Daddy. Who knows? Maybe Rachel won't even tell them about you. Too painful, you know?"

Jay's eyes were blank. Like two marbles stuck on a doll's head.

Harris signalled to the muscle on either side of Jay. "Take him."

"NO!"

The two heavies dragged Jay through the crowd. Through the snow, their feet trampling over the abandoned masks that littered the area. Jay fought but it was a useless struggle. They walked away from the cabin to where the land curved downhill.

There was a road somewhere down there, probably not too far. Most likely, a van was waiting with the engine idling. The back doors would be open, waiting for the cargo so they could leave in a hurry, before the roads succumbed to the weather.

Davie rattled his chair, almost tipped himself over. He called out to Jay. Called out to Harris. He glanced at Iain, lying in a snow coffin. When he looked to the point of descent, he couldn't see Jay. Only the hysterical screams remained, but soon they were gone too, swallowed by the wind.

It felt like hours passed before Harris approached Davie, rifle strap tucked over his shoulder. Alison walked at his side, her arm threaded through his.

Poor Iain, Davie thought. The woman really did a number on him.

Davie wouldn't beg these people for his life, no matter what happened. No matter what they threatened him with, even if it was a fate worse than Jay's. He wouldn't give them the satisfaction.

Elena, I'm sorry.

"You know," Harris said, kneeling down beside the wheelchair. His beard was white, peppered with snowflakes. "Terry and me, we were good friends. Best friends. We were so close back in the day, just like you guys were. We also had a nickname that went around school, just like the Lads did. This was at the start of our academic life, long before the drugs got a hold of us."

He smiled at the recollection.

"Man, we were smart. Terry, he was a wizard at things like maths and chemistry. I'm not just saying that either Davie – we were pretty switched-on kids, way ahead of the pack, you know? Old heads on young shoulders, that's what the teachers said. The kids called us the old boys. Talking fluently about things that mattered: politics, nature, culture. We were interested, we were engaged. We were supposed to do great things."

He wiped the snow off his face.

"I loved Terry like a brother. And it was my fault that everything went wrong. I was the one who brought drugs into our lives. Me."

"Kill me," Davie said, staring out at the fading hills as they disappeared behind the mist. "And get it over with."

Harris blinked fiercely, as if waking up from a dream. He looked at Davie and shook his head.

"I want you to make a decision.

"What?"

"See Davie, you're not the killer. In fact, you're the only one in the cabin who isn't a killer. Jay left me for dead. He let Terry go mad with guilt. As for Iain, well he was willing to burn you alive tonight."

Harris put a hand on Davie's shoulder. Gave it a squeeze.

"I'm a killer too. We're all killers, except you. You didn't kill that woman bud. The one in Argyle Street, you know? Your confession earlier on, it touched me. That took serious balls to lay yourself bare like that. It was genuine. It was real and I appreciate that."

"What do you want?" Davie asked.

"Choose."

"Choose what?"

"It's simple. Live or die."

Davie shook his head in disbelief. "You'd let me live? After what I've just seen?"

"Have I lied to you since you found out the truth?" Harris asked. "What reason have I got to lie now? It's late in the day Davie, and it's your choice. You can go back to London, tell the police everything you know and hope they track us down. Now, if big city police were to show up in Gairloch anytime soon, I'd be amongst the first to know. And if that were to happen, someone from the Hand would take a trip to London immediately. To Croydon, to the house where you and your family live. You understand?"

Davie nodded. Harris wasn't bluffing and he knew it.

"Or," Harris said, "you can go back home, say nothing and live the rest of your life. I have no fight with you bud. It's your choice."

"That's easier said than done."

"Is it?"

"I was supposed to be at Central Station last night," Davie said. "They're already looking for me."

Harris pulled at the tip of his snow-flecked beard. "You're the smart one, that's what Iain said. We can drop you off wherever you like but you'll have to come up with the story about what happened last night. Find a reason, a convincing reason why you weren't there to meet your brother at the train station. That's the best offer you're going to get Davie."

"Why?" Davie said. "Why are you letting me go?"

Alison pointed her rifle at Davie. "If you want to stay with your friends," she said, "just say the word."

Harris reached up, pushed the rifle away. "There doesn't need to be any more bloodshed. Let's clean this mess up and give it a happy ending. What do you say?"

Davie, who'd been so certain of dying, saw the way home. But it came at a terrible price.

"Think of it this way," Harris said, standing up and wiping his coat down again. "Your kids get their dad back. And your wife, her husband. Always remember Davie, when this haunts you further down the line – there was nothing you could have done for Jay and Iain. They were doomed. But your family, they don't need to be."

Harris pointed to the cabin. "In the end, you were the only one who took responsibility for his actions."

He smiled.

"So, what's it to be?"

21

DAVIE
Three weeks later

Davie was upstairs. sitting by the bay window in the spare room.

It was early morning, a little after eight o'clock and he was looking down onto Cherry Avenue, a quiet suburban street in Croydon. Things were happening. The birds were chirping. Cars were backing slowly out of driveways, their drivers bound for work or last-minute Christmas shopping trips.

The snow that had plagued so much of the UK recently hadn't bothered with the south of London. Nonetheless, the pavement around Davie's house would occasionally glisten with frost in the morning. That was enough winter for most people.

Davie sipped his morning coffee. Grateful that he was off work until the day after Boxing Day.

He was dozing off when he heard the sound of a car pulling up outside the house. Felt his nerves jangle. But it was only Frank Taylor, arriving in his flash BMW with his daughter Ruth in the back. They were here to take Davie and Elena's kids, Thomas and Sarah, into the city centre to see Santa Claus in his grotto, their last chance to do so before Christmas Day. The kids had already said their good-byes to Davie. When she came up to see him, Sarah had asked Davie, as she'd often done lately, why Daddy was so sad, especially when it was so close to Christmas. Davie had smiled, told his daughter he was fine and then sent her on her way with a kiss and a hug. Told her not to ask Santa for too much stuff.

It was a relief to be alone.

He listened to Elena downstairs, wrapping the kids up in their winter coats, getting their shoes on. Telling them to calm down, to be careful, not to run on the slippy pavement. With her strong Glasgow accent on show, she hollered a good morning to Frank and Ruth who were waiting in the car.

The Muirs lived in Croydon. Theirs was a fairly humdrum existence of work and child-rearing, punctuated by the occasional social gathering which more often than not, had something to do with work. They were quiet people who mostly kept themselves to themselves and Davie was happy to keep it that way. There was no doubt however, that they were well-liked by their friends and neighbours.

Good people, a colleague had once told Davie over a coffee break. *You and Elena, you're good people.*

After the kids were gone, Elena walked into the upstairs bedroom. She dropped to her knees behind the wheelchair, throwing her arms around Davie's neck.

"Enjoying the view, are we?"

Elena was an attractive, blond-haired woman, two years Davie's junior. She was as sharp as a tack in the brains department, way sharper than he was, and she had the strength of character to compliment her street smarts. She'd been the real hero after the lorry crash turned their lives upside down in 2014. It was Elena who'd pulled Davie back from the abyss. She'd stuck by him, even after he'd begged her in the hospital to leave him. Even after the insults. After he told her that he didn't love her or the kids anymore. But Elena saw through all of his bullshit. Like when Davie told her that he'd kill himself at the first opportunity, she knew that he didn't mean a word of it. Later on, Davie had hated himself for the things he'd said. That was the fear talking – the fear of rejection. He only wanted her to be happy and to live a full life but Elena told him that she could only live a full and happy life with the man that she loved. Legs or no legs. How right she'd been.

Davie Muir was the luckiest man on Earth.

He smirked at the question. "Stunning view? Oh aye. It's taking my breath away."

"It is a little boring, isn't it?" Elena said, glancing at the uninspiring scene outside. "What does that say about us, I wonder? Are we boring?"

"Yep."

She leaned over and kissed him on the cheek.

"You were up early, as usual."

"Couldn't sleep."

Elena straightened up, walked past the chair and perched herself on the window ledge. Now she was facing Davie, a cheerful smile on her face. But Davie knew the smile was a sweetener, preparing him for what was to come.

"Still no news, eh?"

He shook his head. "Nah, nothing."

"Well, it's not been that long. Let's not give up hope yet."

He tried to smile. "I won't."

Davie looked up, saw a tear spilling down her cheek. She quickly rubbed it away and made a face as if reprimanding herself for being silly.

"Och, what an idiot."

Davie's hand went to her leg. "What's wrong darling?"

She waved off the question. "It's nothing. I was just thinking about Jay's fiancée up there in Glasgow. The poor woman, she's pregnant for God's sake and she must be going out of her mind. What you told the police, that's all she's got to go on. That's it. Same with the rest of Jay's family and Iain's family too. What sort of Christmas are they going to have?"

Davie nodded.

Elena was talking about the story. That would be the story of Davie's short-lived kidnapping three weeks ago. The story of how three people had forced him off the London Euston to Glasgow Central train near the border (there was CCTV footage to back this up). How his abductors (who spoke with Cockney accents) told him they were taking him back down to London before drugging him. How at a service station near Penrith, Davie had woken up from the failed dose. How after waking up, he'd found himself in the back of a freezing cold van, screaming for help. How a stranger had opened the back of the van (which was bizarrely unlocked) to find Davie lying on the floor, just as his three kidnappers were making their way across the car park, their arms loaded with supplies for the journey south. How his kidnappers freaked out at the sight of all those people standing around the van. At the sight of the back doors lying wide open. The good Samaritans in the car park got Davie out. The kidnappers, after making a number of threats, had leapt into the van and driven away with the back doors swinging open.

It was the story of a lucky escape.

So far, it had fooled everyone.

What Davie hadn't told the police was how he'd scripted that story with Harris inside a remote cabin in the Highlands. That the kidnappers in the car park were acting out a scene according to his specific instructions.

Davie's story meant the real kidnappers were in the clear. He'd pointed the police in the wrong direction. Told the detectives that one of the kidnappers, prior to putting a needle in his arm, said that the Lads would pay for their crimes. That one of their old classmates was waiting for them down in London. It was to be a private, bloody reunion.

Now, both the Scottish and English police forces were searching for Jay and Iain in the wrong place. Davie's guts churned whenever he thought of the lie and its consequences for others. At the thought of their families, worried sick up there in Glasgow. He still woke up in the middle of the night, reliving the shot that blew Iain's brains out all over the snow. And in those rare moments of silence in the Muir household, when the kids weren't making noise and the dog wasn't barking at passers-by on the street, Davie heard Jay screaming. Screaming as he was led towards an excruciating, unimaginably lonely death.

"We're lucky," Elena said, throwing her arms around Davie again. She peppered his cheek with kisses. Squeezed him so tight that Davie could hardly breathe. "God, how did we get so lucky?"

Davie sat in his chair, breathing in his wife's perfume – an early Christmas present that he'd picked out on a whim.

"I don't know," he said, smiling at her. "I don't know."

That evening, the Muirs were scheduled to go to the Southbank Winter Market – a family tradition they'd kept up since they'd first moved to London and one that Davie usually attended reluctantly. Tonight however, they'd explore the stalls for as long as the others wanted. The kids would overdose on sugar and Davie and Elena would sip a mulled wine under the twinkling lights.

At some point in the evening, Davie would remember to tell his family that he loved them.

THE END

OTHER
THRILLER/HORROR/SUSPENSE
BOOKS BY MARK GILLESPIE

The starlet and the starmaker. It's an age-old story in Hollywood. Now that story's about to be rewritten. In blood.

Scream Test

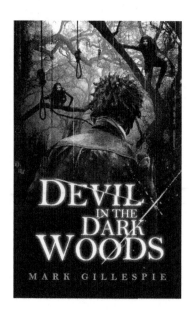

Mike Harvey just broke up with his girlfriend. Now her daddy, the Devil, is coming after him. And Daddy's mad as Hell.

Devil in the Dark Woods

If you love taut, fast-paced, claustrophobic horror, you'll love The Hatching

POST APOCALYPTIC/DYSTOPIAN TITLES BY MARK GILLESPIE

After the End Trilogy

The Exterminators Trilogy

Dystopiaville

The Butch Nolan Trilogy

Mark Gillespie's author website
www.markgillespieauthor.com

Mark Gillespie on Facebook
www.facebook.com/markgillespieswritingstuff

Mark Gillespie on Twitter
www.twitter.com/MarkG_Author

Mark Gillespie on Bookbub
https://www.bookbub.com/profile/mark-gillespie

Printed in Great Britain
by Amazon